"Don't talk, just listen!"

Moira was shouting now, clearly furious. "I know what game you're playing, and it won't work. Marc Rayven has no place in his life for a nondescript little typist. He's out of your league. I'm giving you fair warning. Stay away from him. He belongs to me. Do you understand?"

Feeling defeated, desolate and rejected, Caren Ainsley placed the telephone receiver back on its cradle. Visions of herself and Marc stretched out on the couch, his hands worshiping her body, his lips promising love, blurred before her eyes. Yes, she definitely understood what Moira was saying. Her face flushed a bright scarlet as she thought about what she had almost allowed to happen between herself and Marc. No, that was wrong. He wasn't Marc, he was Mr. Rayven, her employer—nothing more. Regardless of what her heart wanted to believe, regardless of the white heat her body had experienced, Moira was right; Marc Rayven *was* out of Caren's league.

Also available from MIRA Books and
FERN MICHAELS

PAINT ME RAINBOWS

Coming soon

WHISPER MY NAME
January 1999

FERN
NIGHTSTAR
MICHAELS

MIRA

ISBN 1-55166-458-5

NIGHTSTAR

NIGHTSTAR

One

Whoever coined the phrase "Blue Monday" had certainly known what he was talking about, Caren Ainsley thought morosely from her desk in the typing pool of Rayven Cosmetics. It was raining in New York City proverbial cats and dogs, and had been for several days. The rent was due in two days, and if this weather continued, she wouldn't be able to make her class at the community college where she was enrolled in a secretarial course.

Impatiently, Caren brushed at a feather of hair that kept eluding the tight bun at the back of her head. She frowned and her glasses slipped down on her nose. Darn it, when were her contacts going to be ready? She frowned again. Even if they were ready today it would be another three weeks before she could save the money to pay for them. She brightened momentarily when she visualized the day she would get them and then, voilà, she would be an instant beauty with gorgeous men throwing themselves at her feet. She would also get a new hairdo, of course, to go with the fantastic job she would have once she had finished her secretarial course in a few weeks.

A new life, sort of. Off with the old Caren and on with the new. She shouldn't be thinking about that now, not with all the work sitting unfinished on her desk. It was Secretary Week, or so the sign hanging in the outer office said. With all the secretaries at Rayven Cosmetics out to a fantastic lunch, she was holding down the fort, along with her supervisor, Maggie Bryant.

"Caren, stop what you're doing and come with me," ordered an agitated voice from behind the partition in the long typing-pool room. "Hurry, please."

"What is it, Miss Bryant? Did I do something wrong?" Caren asked in a fearful voice.

"Good heavens no, child. On the contrary, you've done something right by taking that secretarial course. It's going to pay off for you right now. Listen to me carefully, Caren. As you know, all of the secretaries are attending the company lunch in their honor, but right now there's a board meeting going on, and Marc

Rayven just called down for a secretary to sit in. I'm giving you your chance for promotion, Caren. I've seen your stenographic skills, and I know that you're the fastest typist, not to mention the most accurate, in the pool. If you do a good job now, you might be able to move up to a better position instead of looking elsewhere for a job once your course is finished. You have to hurry. Mr. Rayven is not known for his patience, and you know all about his assistant, Moira. If you're even moments late, she would have no compunction about slicing you to ribbons—in front of all the board members,'' Maggie Bryant said in somber tones.

"But, Miss Bryant, I've never met any of those people. I'm not sure I'm good enough or fast enough to handle this. Are you sure there isn't someone else?"

"Caren, there is no one else. Look around. You know the other girls will be out longer for lunch today. And the only reason you didn't go to the park to eat was because you didn't want to go out in the rain. If you give up this lunch hour, I'll allow you to leave an hour early this evening. Or another day for that matter. Please say you'll do it. I think you can handle it,'' the older woman said firmly.

"But...but look how I'm dressed. If I had known, I would have worn a suit or something," Caren protested.

"You look tailored and that's all that matters. A navy-blue skirt and white tailored blouse is fitting in any office. Don't worry, I spoke with Mr. Rayven myself and told him I was sending you, and I explained that you were almost finished with your course. I recommended you so highly, Caren, that you can't let me down now."

"All right, I'll do it, but I'll have butterflies in the pit of my stomach the whole time. I need a steno pad and some sharp pencils. Walk with me to the conference room, Miss Bryant?"

Caren took a deep breath and stared at her reflection in the window. She looked plain— plain and neat. She brushed back a stray wisp of soft brown hair from her brow and nudged her heavy-rimmed glasses back on her nose. Horror of horrors, her hands were shaking. How could she take dictation? She couldn't. Yes, she could, and she would! She was at the head of her class, and if Maggie Bryant had faith in her ability, that was enough for her.

Another deep breath. Marc Rayven. She was actually going to sit at the conference table and take down his dictation and notes of the meeting.

Wait till the other girls in the typing pool heard this. Handsome, debonair, and don't forget, dashing, she told herself; Marc Rayven, president and chairman of the board of Rayven Cosmetics, was all these things.

The profile she had read just a few short months ago in the Sunday supplement said he was a thirty-five-year-old genius and well on his way to building an empire in the cosmetics industry. The article had hinted at a new, top-secret line of cosmetics that would either place Rayven at the top of the business or at the bottom. The article had gone on to cite quotes from the other prominent figures in the industry, and Caren had been amazed to find Rayven described as "ruthless," "mercenary," a "playboy," and in other terms far less complimentary.

"Here you go, Caren, three fresh pencils and a brand new steno book. Hurry, you have only a few minutes. I want you in there before the meeting gets under way. Make me proud of you, Caren," the older woman said fondly. With a last gentle pat on her shoulder, Maggie withdrew, leaving Caren to stand alone in front of the closed conference-room door.

Moistening her dry lips, Caren knocked softly and then took a step backward. Moira Evans opened the door, her patrician features haughty and aloof. "You must be Miss Ainsley. We've been waiting for you." She made it sound like "we" had been waiting for *hours!* Caren glanced around. The board members weren't seated and Marc Rayven was not in attendance. Caren's head went up a little higher as she stood quietly, waiting to be told where she was to sit. She was getting a headache. The perfume Moira Evans was wearing was not going to sit well with Caren. It was overpowering, heady to the point of being sickening. She knew it wasn't a Rayven perfume. Rayven perfumes were all subtle, yet alluring, and they didn't overpower the way Moira's scent was doing.

"Sit here, Miss Ainsley," Moira said motioning to a chair next to the head of the table.

Caren quietly advanced across the room to take her assigned seat at the long conference table.

Moira Evans dismissed Caren with a nod. "Ladies, gentlemen, please be seated. Marc, Mr. Rayven, asked me to get the meeting under way. He's going to be a few minutes late as you can see."

Chairs were pulled out from the incredibly long, polished table as the board members took their seats. Cigarettes were lit, pads and pencils shifted from one spot to another. Muted conversations wafted through the high vaulted room as Caren made herself nearly comfortable in the plush high-backed chair at one end of the gleaming table. In spite of her resolution to appear efficient and experienced, Caren's eyes began to wander from the soft celery-green carpet that practically swallowed your ankles when you walked on it to the even softer-colored celery-green walls that rose majestically to the fifteen-foot ceilings. A corner office, it had two walls of wraparound glass; through filmy yards of draperies, these walls displayed an exquisite view of New York's East Side. Along the other two sides of the rectangular room were low white sofas and before them stood heavy, square, glass cocktail tables. The only splashes of color came from the Manet paintings hung above the sofas, illuminated by their own gleaming brass lights.

Moira Evans stood at the head of the conference table waiting until the members of the board realized that she was not going to speak until she had their undivided attention. Caren had to admire the woman's poise as she stood there, still as a statue, eyes flashing, mouth grim. Eventually, the room stilled.

Caren waited expectantly, her pencil poised, ready to begin her notes of the meeting. There was no doubt in her mind that Moira Evans belonged in a cosmetics firm. The woman's makeup was perfection and the expensive Halston suit she wore molded her slim form perfectly, its willow gray outlining her incredibly slim figure. Every jet-black hair was in its place, swinging freely about her face and ending bluntly just above the snow-white collar of her Oscar de la Renta blouse. Every male eye in the room was on Marc Rayven's assistant; Moira knew it and preened beneath it. The woman nodded her head to acknowledge the silence and prepared to speak from a sheaf of papers held in her manicured hand. It appeared to Caren as though this was Miss Evans' grand moment, a moment she had anticipated and relished. She was going to bring a meeting to order in place of the company's president.

Suddenly the conference-room doors swung open as if some unleashed hurricane had made landfall. A whirlwind entered in its wake in the personage of Marc Rayven. He waved airily at the assembled board and motioned with one hand for Moira to stand aside. What a pity, Caren thought uncharitably, Miss Evans' grand moment dashed to splinters by the entrance of a hurricane.

Marc Rayven was imposing, an electric personality. He threw himself into his chair at the head of the table. "I'll take it from here, Moira." His voice was clipped, cool, professional. For one instant Moira stiffened and Caren expected her to defend her position at the head of the table. Apparently, Miss Evans thought better of it and gracefully took her seat across from Caren.

Rayven shuffled his papers and then lifted his head to stare at Caren. He frowned and Caren's heart fluttered. "You must be the secretary."

"This is the girl who'll take the minutes of the meeting, Marc," Moira said coolly as she stared straight into Caren's eyes.

Caren's shoulders straightened. "My name is Caren Ainsley, Mr Rayven; I'm from the typing pool." Caren spoke quietly, surprised that her voice was so confident.

"Now I remember; Maggie spoke to me about you. I won't need you after all. But take a seat just in case."

"Thank you, Mr. Rayven." Caren melted

when he smiled down at her. It was almost as if the room were empty and they had a secret between them. It was that kind of smile, she decided.

As he prepared his notes, Caren watched him. He was handsome, more so than his pictures in the society columns. How aptly named he was, with his hair the black of a raven's wing. And his eyes were deep blue, almost turquoise. A definitely handsome combination, she mused. Evidently, Moira thought so too because Caren was receiving the most malevolent look she had ever received in her life. And that look could mean only one thing. *Moira Evans saw Marc Rayven as her special property.*

Caren relaxed. Moira Evans couldn't do anything to her. Not here in this conference room or outside it either for that matter. She didn't know how she knew, she just knew that Marc Rayven would protect her. Whoever the journalist was who had said he was ruthless didn't know this Marc Rayven. So much for profiles in Sunday supplements.

Leaning back in his chair and tossing the stack of papers he was holding onto the shining surface of the table, Marc Rayven spoke. "Let me begin by saying that this is not a formal meeting.

I would prefer at this time to consider it a sort of open discussion." He waited for comment. When none was forthcoming, he continued. "I say that we go with the enfleurage method for the new perfume line. I know," he said holding up his hand to quell the disagreements, "it's the most expensive method, but this is a one-of-a-kind perfume. If we use distillation, we'll end up selling it to the dime stores. I want all of you to think along the lines of an entire line—from cosmetics to toiletries to perfume—all bearing the same name. I want this scent on every woman in America. I want them talking about it. I want it blitzed from one end of the country to the other. After we do that, we'll tackle the foreign markets, but this is an *American* perfume, made by an *American* manufacturer and at this time we're aiming exclusively for the *American* woman. A woman like Caren Ainsley." His gaze fell on her and something in it warmed her cheeks. "We're going to give the American woman," he continued, "a line of her own—cologne, toilet water, lipsticks, bath powders, and oils.

"You other ladies," he said, addressing the female members of the board, "can afford to pamper yourselves with expensive French perfumes. But it's time we began to think of the average American woman. She's got as much right as the rest of you to want a scent that's within her means. And I plan to give it to her. Let's kick it around a little. What we want is a perfume with sensitivity, a perfume that wears for all seasons. Most of all, we want a scent that becomes a woman's own the instant she puts it on."

"That's impossible, Marc," one of the men at the other end of the table insisted.

"At one time I would have agreed with you, but not now. My chemists have come up with something I think is going to blow this industry sky-high. I have here a sample and I want all of you to test it. Tell me, ladies and gentlemen, if you think we have the right mixture of spice, wood, floral, and fruit all rolled up into one. A complete line. Dollars in your bank accounts. Not just perfume, an entire line."

Caren watched in amazement as Marc Rayven bent down to his attaché case to withdraw a small, slender vial. Tenderly, he removed the cork stopper and inhaled deeply, then passed the vial to Moira, who sniffed and passed it along, too. There were murmurs of appreciation and approval.

The man sitting beside Caren passed the vial to her. Cautiously, she sniffed and then sniffed again. "It's beautiful, I've never experienced anything like it."

Marc lapsed into thought for a moment, then slapped his palm on the conference tale. "That's it! Did you hear what she just said?" He inclined his head in Caren's direction. "She said she'd never experienced anything like it! This is more than a perfume! It's an *experience!* An experience I have decided to call Nightstar. Our promotions will say: Nightstar—an experience."

"Now wait a moment, Marc," came a sober, dissenting voice from the far end of the table.

"Burgess?" Marc addressed the man. "You have a problem with the name of Nightstar?"

"No, no, it's a lovely name. Perfect as a matter of fact." The elderly gentleman smiled and bowed in Caren's direction. "As I see it, the problems still exist in reaching the American woman."

"Burgess, as head of our internal publicity department, your word carries weight with me. Why don't you just spit it out. What's your problem?"

The slim gray-haired man whom Marc Rayven called Burgess straightened his shoulders and addressed the board. "It's a wonderful idea. The problem, as I see it, exists in promotion. If Rayven Cosmetics sticks to the perfume and *only* the perfume, there is no problem in having our campaign ready for the coming Christmas season. Christmas being the most popular time of year for buying fragrance. Gifts and—"

"Just get to the point, Burgess," Marc interrupted.

"The point is, *in promoting the perfume,* we can hire a high-fashion model to do our advertising. *In creating a whole line for the American woman,* a high-fashion model just wouldn't go down, if you know what I mean. She would be associated in the public's mind with money, designer labels, and unfortunately, expensive toiletries. These will be mundane, affordable items; and yet the products require the glamour these models portray. It would take months to map out the kind of campaign that would deliver the message that this scent is for the average American woman. For the secretaries and the housewives and even for the little shop girls who'll sell the stuff. That would take a great deal of thought and, quite frankly, Marc, I don't believe there is anyone who could conceive of such a campaign. Others have tried and failed as you well know.

It would be easier to get Mickey Mouse elected President.''

Marc sat back in his chair, his sun-bronzed hands running through his hair while he considered Burgess' words.

When he lifted his head, he stared unflinchingly down the table at Burgess. "I agree with you completely. But you see I have no intention of using high-fashion models. I don't see some scrawny woman with good bones becoming the identity of the American woman. We need an amateur!''

"Marc, that's impossible and you know it! *All* the companies use professional models. Professional people. We have too much at stake to use anyone but a professional who knows her business. I'm afraid we're going to have to go with the perfume only. Perhaps at a later date—'' Burgess said confidently, knowing Rayven encouraged his executives to speak their minds; and it was an informal meeting.

"No way. I say we go with the whole line. I believe in it. I'm telling you that the Nightstar line will be accepted by American women. Loved by them. *If* we take one from their ranks and make her our Nightstar spokeperson. We *can't* use the same old approach. Women have to *believe* that Nightstar can make them be the women they want to be.'' His turquoise eyes flew around the room and landed on Caren, who was watching him wide-eyed. ''Take Caren here. Who is she? A typist in a company pool. But who is she when she goes home at night? Who does she dream of becoming? And the same goes for the women who work at home. Who do they want to be? That's the message that Nightstar has to convey. 'Be the woman you've always dreamed of being... Nightstar becomes *You*....'''

Caren was listening attentively. Marc Rayven seemed to know so much about women, all women. He even knew about her. He knew that in her fantasies she was never a typist. No, she was a slave girl kidnapped by a handsome sheik...Scarlett O'Hara...Shakespeare's Juliet....

''We all know you've always had a flair for advertising, Marc, but you must see it is not feasible to install a complete Nightstar line. This has got to be thought out thoroughly.''

Marc glared down the table looking at each and every individual board member. ''Do you want Nightstar or don't you? Either we go with the complete line or it's 'no go.'''

"But where will we find the production company? The models?"

"*No models.* We need Miss Jane Doe. Nightstar will become *her* perfume, *her* image, *her* fantasy."

Burgess spoke up again. "Marc. Be reasonable. All that Jane Doe stuff makes good copy, not good sense. Of course you need a professional model. You can't just take a girl off the street and make her your Nightstar girl."

"If I believe in this line, I can. Can't you see, if we use a model, someone whose face has been seen in every fashion magazine in America, how are we going to convince women that they *too* can be a Nightstar girl? No, we need someone who's an unknown.... We need that girl off the street." Marc Rayven's eyes raked every face in the room, resting inordinately long on Caren's. "We don't have to find a girl off the street," he said softly. "The girl fresh out of the typing pool would do just as well. Miss Ainsley," he said firmly, "how would you like to become our Nightstar girl?"

Gasps filled the room. "Marc! You can't," Moira Evans cried.

"Have you lost your mind?" said someone from one end of the conference table.

"Make sense, man." Burgess sighed, exasperated.

"I haven't lost my mind.... I am making sense. Why not?" Rayven defended. "She's a woman, isn't she? She has two arms, two legs.... Her figure is trim and neat—"

"But her hair!" a female member moaned.

"And those glasses—"

"It will never work."

Caren was dumbfounded and then paralyzed as she listened to the rousing protests directed at Marc Rayven. They were picking her apart as though she were an object, not a woman with feelings.

"She must be twenty-five or twenty-six, at least. Too old."

"We need someone with a sense of style...."

On and on they found her faults, leaving her flushed, stricken, breathless. Oh, God, if she could only crawl under the table and hide until they all went away. She didn't want to be the Nightstar girl.... She wanted to finish her course at the community college and find a nice job somewhere.

"She has no sense of style. Marc, we need someone who can bring something to Nightstar—"

"And *I* say that the Nightstar line can make a woman anyone she wants to be," Marc Rayven thundered. "And I say we go with Caren Ainsley."

"Marc, be reasonable," Moira's voice cajoled. "Call off the joke. Tell everyone you've been joking."

Silence pervaded the room. Moira Evans was giving Rayven an out from his ridiculous idea.

"I *am* being reasonable. Caren is the kind of girl we see every day. She's not a beauty queen. She's a hard-working, level-headed girl. Just like the kind of girls and women who will buy Nightstar—the kind of woman who can't be fooled. I know she's not perfect. If she were, she'd be one of the professional models I definitely do not want for Nightstar. We're going to prove that we can make a silk purse from a sow's ear."

Caren looked up. Had Mr. Rayven said that? Had he called her a sow's ear? Horrified at the thought of being so demeaned, her shoulders stiffened and a hot flush of anger stained her cheeks.

"Do I have to remind you all that as president and chairman of the board, I own the controlling interest in this company? Your affirmative votes would be most welcome, but they are not necessary. Anyone who so chooses can offer his stock in this company for sale. I'll be glad to take it off his hands at current market prices.''

Hush was the only word that came to Caren's mind. It was so still one could have heard a pin drop on the thickly carpeted floor.

''If Miss Ainsley agrees, she will be our new Nightstar girl.'' Marc Rayven left his place at the head of the table and stood beside Caren. He took her hands in his own and looked down into her face. His remarkable blue eyes melted into her own; her breath came in little gasps. She was frightened, embarrassed. She wanted to run, never to see the inside of Rayven Cosmetics again. But Marc Rayven's hands were holding her, and he was looking down into her face. There was such a silent persuasion there, a hope. How could she, after all she had heard, agree to his wishes? She knew that the others felt his scheme would fail. Could she play such a major part in that failure? Could she be the Nightstar girl? It could mean the end to her financial hassles and provide an escape from the humdrum to life in the fast lane. Before she realized what she was doing, she nodded her agreement.

''Caren Ainsley, you are our Nightstar girl.

From this moment on your life will change. Your dreams will come true."

Caren was stunned. The board members were looking at her with respect, if not approval. Was Marc Rayven making a joke at her expense? One glance at Moira Evans' face told her the head of the cosmetics firm was deadly serious. It couldn't be. This just couldn't be happening to her. One moment she was Caren Ainsley, typing-pool worker, and the next she was the Nightstar girl.

"But I only came in here to take dictation. This is so sudden—"

"Forget the dictation. Miss Caren Ainsley, I'm going to take you out to lunch and buy you the biggest steak on the menu. Now, this minute. Get your coat and while you're at it, quit your job. You were just promoted. Tell Maggie to get in touch with me later this afternoon."

Caren left the board room in a daze, Moira Evans' eyes stabbing her every step of the way. The minute the door closed behind her, she ran as if the hounds of hell were at her heels. She wanted to run away from Rayven Cosmetics—run so far she could pretend she'd never heard the name Nightstar, run away from Marc Rayven who could make her agree to change her whole life.

Two

Some of the girls in the typing pool were jealous at the news, others were genuinely happy for her. Lunch with the gorgeous president of Rayven Cosmetics! Lunch with Marc Rayven!

"Yes, she's leaving us!" Maggie Bryant cried happily. "She's going to work for Mr. Rayven himself. Isn't that right, Caren?"

Caren nodded, still too stunned to speak.

"You'd better hurry, child, run along to the washroom and powder your nose. You said Mr. Rayven didn't want to be kept waiting," Maggie said, literally pulling Caren away from her co-workers.

Caren found her voice. "I don't believe this is happening to me. I simply don't believe it! I'm going, Miss Bryant, but I'll be back after lunch and give you all the details."

"Fine, fine. Hurry along now; you really can't keep Mr. Rayven waiting, and your nose is on the shiny side,'' Maggie responded as she thrust open the door that led to the corridor. ''Just a minute,'' Maggie said drawing Caren aside. ''I think you should know the office grapevine has it that Moira Evans has her cap set on being Rayven Cosmetics' first lady, and the way things have been going lately it looks to be more true than untrue. In short, honey, Moira wants to be Mrs. Marc Rayven. Any way you look at it, you are going to be a threat to her. Be careful,'' she admonished in a tight little whisper.

Embracing Maggie, Caren then raced off to the lounge area. She stopped momentarily as she fished around in her handbag for lipstick and compact. She was off to the side unable to see into the area where the washbasins were. She would think about Maggie's words later. She heard voices and running water. At first, she paid no attention to the voices, and if the truth were known, she simply didn't want to come down off that fluffy cloud she was on to hear everyday words.

She, Caren Ainsley, was going to be Marc Rayven's Nightstar girl, and that definitely took her out of the humdrum. She blinked when she happened to hear her name mentioned and then smiled. News of her promotion had traveled quickly.

"I don't know why Marc did what he did. But that ugly duckling has no more of a chance of being the Nightstar girl than Maggie Bryant. I was there, remember? I had dinner with Marc last night and he was boasting to me, boasting mind you, that he could convince the board that he could find the most wretched excuse for a woman and make her into his new Nightstar girl—with the proper promotion and buildup. But I didn't take him seriously!"

Caren's world literally crumbled at her feet. The voice belonged to Moira Evans. Marc Rayven couldn't have said those things. He just couldn't have said them!

A second voice seemed as questioning as Caren felt. "Moira, that's an awful thing to say about anyone. You make it sound as though Mr. Rayven *handpicked* this girl to be his victim. I can't believe Mr. Rayven would say something like that. I'm sorry, I just don't believe it."

"Well, you'd better believe it, Lorraine. If you want proof, just ask little Miss Four-Eyes if she took down one word of dictation. Not one squiggly line," Moira said triumphantly. "Marc said it himself when he told the others that she, the typist or whatever she is, was just what he was waiting for. He set her up. The whole board knows it and so do I. The little dummy fell for it, too.''

Caren was stunned. She had to get out of here, out of this lounge area, before Moira Evans and her secretary came out of the powder room. There was no way she would allow that Evans woman to see what her callous words had done to her.

Quietly, Caren opened the door. She would quit her job all right. She would quit Rayven Cosmetics altogether and go somewhere else. How could that man make a fool of her like this? The words from the Sunday supplement ricocheted in her brain. *Ruthless, mercenary.* Ruthless people trampled over other people and paid no attention to their feelings. Mercenary people were concerned with money night and day. Ruthless and mercenary. Tears rose to the surface. She had to get out of here. Run! her mind screamed. Don't let him humiliate you. Moira Evans wouldn't say such brutal things without truth. Or would she?

''Here you are. Maggie said you were powdering your nose. You look fine, Caren,'' Marc Rayven said gallantly.

Now, what was she going to do? She couldn't run now; she felt too ashamed, too humiliated, and all the girls on the floor were waving and giggling. Even Maggie wore an ear-to-ear grin. She had to go through with the lunch, but she didn't have to take the job. She knew how to say no. She looked up at the tall man towering over her and forced a sickly smile to her lips. "Yes, I'm about as ready as I'll ever be," she answered in an even tone that surprised even herself.

"Then we should be on our way. I called down to have the doorman have a taxi waiting. No point in taking my car out of the garage. How does the Russian Tea Room sound to you?"

Caren had heard of the elegant restaurant, but had never been fortunate enough to eat there, either as someone's guest or on her own. New York City boasted many fine restaurants, but the Russian Tea Room was supposed to be somewhere near the top of the list. How she would have enjoyed it if she hadn't heard Moira's hateful words.

"A penny for your thoughts, Caren," Marc murmured as he helped her into the back of a Checker cab.

"I'm sorry; I was thinking of something. What was it you asked me?" she said leaning back in the leather seat.

"I asked you how the Russian Tea Room sounded to you?"

It seemed to Caren that there was a slight edge to Marc's words. "I think it's fine. I've never been there, but I have certainly heard of it. Isn't it a little late to get reservations?" Caren asked peering at her watch.

Caren was pleased that her escort suddenly wore a sheepish look. "It is, but I called ahead and pulled a few strings. We won't have a problem."

"You just called ahead and everything was arranged? Just like that?" Caren asked in amazement.

Marc Rayven grinned. "Actually, there was a bit more to it than that, but it doesn't matter as long as everything's set."

Caren flinched as the Sunday supplement swam before her eyes. Playboy, rich playboy. Rich playboy escorts ugly duckling to famous restaurant. Why not? Why should she care what he thought of her? Imperceptibly, she drew away from him, more aware of him as a man than anything else. Suddenly, she felt confused. He didn't seem to be the kind of man who would say the kind of things Moira said.

"Are you always this quiet, Caren? By the way," he continued, not waiting for her to reply, "call me Marc. I really feel as though we're going to get to know each other very well. I wonder why that is?" he mused.

Caren's defenses rose. She wouldn't answer that or any of the other questions he asked. She shielded herself; the person who did that didn't get hurt. She knew instinctively that the man sitting next to her could hurt her—hurt her badly if she allowed it.

Marc Rayven whisked Caren from the cab and into the restaurant so fast her head was spinning. She watched with an amused expression as Marc spoke with a tall, dark-haired man. He motioned to the top floor and Caren heard the words "by the window." Within seconds they were seated at a table overlooking busy Fifty-seventh Street.

Caren ordered white wine and Marc ordered Scotch and soda. They sipped, eyeing each other. "Why do I keep getting the feeling that you don't approve of me?" Marc asked in a cool tone.

"I can't imagine why you would think that," Caren replied bringing the glass to her lips.

"I have a habit of doing things very fast. I've done so all my life. I make a decision and then I follow it through to the end. Some of my competitors frown on what they call my 'unorthodox methods' but they have never failed me as yet."

They made small talk, each eyeing the other warily, or so Caren thought. What in the world did he think she was thinking? Better yet, what was *he* thinking? Was she supposed to be all bubbly and excited? Evidently. And now when she was keeping a low profile, he couldn't understand it. Ugly duckling! Somewhere between the wine and the end of the appetizer, Caren made up her mind to go through with Marc Rayven's plan for her. Why not? She didn't have anything to lose. If he wanted to consider her some kind of test case, some kind of guinea pig to practice on, why not let him? As long as he paid her more than what she was making in the typing pool, it was all right with her.

"Have you always worn glasses, Caren?" Marc asked bluntly. "Let me see what you look like without them."

"I've worn them for the past several years. In the beginning it was just to read or study, but yes, to answer your unasked questions, I do need them to see. I ordered a pair of contact lenses several weeks ago, and I expect them any day now," Caren said evenly, striving to keep her tone neutral. She removed the square, dark-rimmed glasses and stared at Marc Rayven.

"Your eyes are incredible, just the perfect shade of lavender. Did you know Elizabeth Taylor has eyes the same color as yours?"

Caren smiled in spite of herself. "That was a superb compliment. You could have said I had eyes like Elizabeth Taylor instead of the other way around."

Marc grinned. "Now that you mention it, I see what you mean. I don't know Elizabeth Taylor, but I do know you. It seemed natural to say it that way."

"Whatever," Caren said sipping at the wine.

"Tell me, Caren, do you have any ties keeping you here in the big city? We will probably need you to go on the road to help promote the line and I want to know now if there will be any kind of difficulties."

Caren forced her tone to be neutral. "I'm quite alone. My father was in the military, but he died a year ago. I have no other family. I'm world-traveled, if that will set your mind at ease. I see no problems, do you?"

"No boyfriends who will gnash their teeth if

you desert them?'' His blue eyes challenged. Was it her imagination or had the man's tone softened somewhat?

''No one in particular, if that's what you mean. I didn't know men gnashed their teeth; I just thought women did that when they got angry. At a man, of course.'' Caren smiled.

''Then it would appear we're in business. You will shortly become Rayven Cosmetics' Nightstar girl. Tomorrow morning, you're to report to me; and Moira Evans, my assistant, will see to your transformation.''

Caren swallowed hard. She knew somehow that it would be Moira.

''I would like to ask a question. What does an assistant do? I'm referring to Miss Evans.'' She couldn't bring herself to say Moira's name to the man sitting across from her.

''Quite a few things as a matter of fact. For the most part she's a buffer between me and others. She has not only a feel but also a flair for the cosmetic business. She had her own boutique for a good many years. She has very good business sense and she's been a good friend and sounding board.''

She couldn't keep sipping at the nearly empty wineglass. What to do with her nervous hands?

This time there was no mistake; there had been a fond note in his voice when he said Moira was a good friend. Playboys always had gorgeous girls around, she thought glumly.

"All in all, she's fairly close to being perfect. It's strange how she can almost anticipate my needs."

Caren nearly choked. "Are you saying she's without faults? I never met anyone like that." This time there was a definite edge to her voice. Marc Rayven sensed it and his eyes narrowed.

"Let's just say she has a few imperfect character traits."

"And I'm the ugly duckling you're going to transform into a beautiful swan." Caren grimaced as she plunged her fork into the thick steak she didn't want and knew she couldn't eat.

Caren watched, fascinated at the way Marc cut his steak. He had strong, square, capable-looking hands. She wondered if they would be gentle if they ever got close enough to touch her. A bright flush stained her cheeks, and she was glad Marc was intent on his food and didn't notice. She couldn't get out of line, think things that would never come into being. He was offering her a job and she was accepting it—pure and simple, a job. Nothing would come of it.

Not if her intuition was right about Moira Evans' possessive eyes when they fell on Marc. And always remember, she cautioned herself, that I am the ugly duckling. I must never lose sight of that. And last of all, but not least, Moira would always be in the wings reminding her, lest she forget.

Each second that brought Caren closer to the Rayven Cosmetics firm left her feeling more trapped. Why was she going through with all of this? Why was she subjecting herself to Moira's sure-to-come insults and Marc Rayven's desire to turn her from an ugly duckling into a beautiful swan? *Hopefully* a beautiful swan.

Rayven Cosmetics was less than half a block away when a strong gust of wind snatched her crushed-velvet beret from her head. Giving her hat up for lost, she braced herself against the buffeting wind and hurried for the door that would lead her to her new duties.

She felt the light touch on her shoulder and then heard the words. For a moment she did not comprehend who was doing the talking and touching. "Your little hat gave me a hell of a time, but I'm a kite flyer from way back. I was right behind you when that wind blew up and I saw it go sailing. I leaped into the air and there it was, right on the end of a street sign.''

"Mr....Mr. Rayven. You didn't have to do that. I wouldn't want to make you late. I gave up on the hat. But thank you,'' Caren muttered, not certain what else she should say to the tall man grinning down at her.

"Of course, I had to do it. I couldn't leave a lady in distress now, could I? And I'm not late for work. Did you forget? I'm the boss.'' He gave her a devastating smile. "Actually, I walk in the morning. There's something about greeting each day with a brisk walk.''

Caren lengthened her steps to match the long-legged stride of the man walking alongside her. She couldn't believe the twist her life was taking. Here was the president of Rayven Cosmetics talking to her as though they were old friends. Sure they were, she thought cynically. All he was interested in was promoting his cosmetics and keeping on the good side of her.

A small warning system in Caren's brain went off and the smile died on her lips. Over and over it repeated the message. He's not interested in ducklings, just swans who can make pots of money for his firm and make him *numero uno* in the cosmetics industry. Well, she didn't have to go along. During her transformation she would have to do as she was told in order to earn her pay. Outside of the office and the glamorous salons, she would let him know she saw right through his little plan—thanks to having overheard Miss Evans in the lavatory.

Caren hadn't realized she had ceased walking until the feathery light touch startled her for a second time. "Do revolving doors hold some kind of terror for you?" Rayven's cool voice demanded. "Is something wrong? I've been speaking to you, but I don't think you've heard a word I said."

Caren stepped into the opening, and before she realized it, she was standing next to Marc Rayven. At best, it was cramped. A flush stained Caren's cheeks when she stared up at Marc and noted the strange look on his face. "If I could bottle the color on your cheeks, I would make a fortune."

Caren flushed a deeper crimson. Why was she forever doing such stupid things? Now he was looking at her as though she had two heads. Two-headed ladies didn't do much for the cosmetics business. He was probably sorry he had made such a hasty decision in hiring her. If ever there was a time to say something brilliant, this was it. Moira would know exactly what to say and just how to say it. On the other hand, Moira would never, never, under any circumstances enter a revolving door with someone else. Caren could almost hear the musical tone, "But darling, one simply doesn't do that! Infants, toddlers, perhaps; adults never but never, darling."

Caren forced a sickly smile to her lips. "I guess I wasn't thinking or watching where I was going." It sounded lame and she knew it. Marc Rayven's face still wore that strange look.

"If you're sure you're all right, I'm going to leave you here." He seemed genuinely concerned. "I'm meeting someone in the coffee shop."

A second later she felt a careless kind of kiss on her high cheekbone. Not exactly careless, to her it seemed more insolent. Annoyed at herself and even more annoyed with the Nightstar King, as she now referred to him in her mind, Caren stalked off to the waiting elevator and marched inside, her face a vivid scarlet.

Caren fixed her gaze on the overhead number plate and wished the pesky elevator would go on forever. Sooner or later it was going to stop at the thirtieth floor, and she would have to get out. A frightening feeling of dread was making her feel all trembly and weightless. Was any job worth all of this turmoil? Was Marc Rayven worth all this heart fluttering? A Nightstar girl should be in control. It was too late to worry now. The elevator door was opening with a silent swoosh and then she was standing in the reception area, feeling like a lost lamb. Squaring her shoulders, she announced herself to the receptionist. Then she affixed a grim, tight look to her mouth and marched down the corridor to where Moira Evans awaited. "And the lamb goes to the slaughter," Caren muttered to herself.

Moira was a commercial artist's dream in her burgundy dress. To Caren's inexperienced eye it looked like nothing more than sheer handkerchiefs sewn together with the points hanging and swishing sensuously about her elegant knees. A wide gold braided belt and a slender gold chain were her only accessories. Caren was impressed. It was also evident that Moira was not impressed with her new protégée. She gave the appearance of dusting her hands and looking helplessly about. Caren could almost read her thoughts. "Whatever am I going to do with this infant?"

A devil of impishness perched itself on

Caren's shoulders. "Mold me, Miss Evans, into the Nightstar girl. I'm all yours."

Moira Evans moistened her glossy lips, which were just a shade lighter than her dress, and stared at the slender girl. Her voice was arrogant, haughty. "There's just *so* much I can do! Follow me, please."

She dresses like a model and walks like a model. If she can turn me into a close second, perhaps I won't dislike her so much, Caren thought with feeling. But do I *really* want to be like her? She answered her own question. Of course not. I just want... Actually, what I would like to have is her beau. Such an old-fashioned term. Marc Rayven could hardly be called a beau. He was Moira's man. They were an item, a thing, according to the grapevine and Maggie, and there must be truth in it because Maggie didn't indulge in idle gossip. Her warning to Caren echoed clearly. They appeared to have a relationship other than the one that went on in the office. Surely they didn't live together! And if they did, what business was it of hers? The only way it could be her business was if she made it her business and that was the one thing she had no intention of doing.

Moira's tone was curt and cold. "Wait here," was the command.

Caren seated herself primly on a vivid orange chair and waited. Just where did Moira think she was going to go? she wondered tartly. She liked this whole situation less every moment. Caren watched as Moira stood inside the doorway, talking in soft whispers. Every so often she waved her hands in a languid kind of gesture to emphasize a point she was obviously trying to make. Whatever she was trying to do, the man seemed to object. From time to time he glanced in Caren's direction, and then shook his head negatively.

The gold leaf on the door said the salon was operated by Jacques Duval. It was the makeup salon, evidently the one all the models used. Caren watched in alarm as Jacques stepped back a step and finally nodded his head. Apparently, he was finally agreeing to whatever demand Moira was making. Agreeing, but not liking whatever he was agreeing to do. Moira's face was now wreathed in smiles as she made her way back to where Caren waited, but not before she pecked Jacques on the cheek.

"I'm leaving you here in Jacques' capable hands. He'll call down for me when he's finished with you. Mr. Rayven wants hourly reports on your progress.'' Her pale blue eyes glittered and her handkerchief-like hem swirled angrily around Moira's legs as she stalked from the salon's tiny foyer.

Caren inhaled deeply. Now she was in someone else's hands. Hourly reports! A sigh caught in her throat as she awaited Monsieur Jacques.

At the end of three hours, Caren felt as though she'd been pushed through a gristmill, but she did notice a sense of excitement begin to well up in her at the astonished looks of the people who were "doing her over." They all, with the exception of Jacques Duval, seemed to be enjoying her transformation into Rayven's Nightstar girl.

Although she had barely moved a muscle that morning, she felt achy and exhausted. First order of the day had been a body massage, a steam bath, and then another massage; after which her eyebrows had been painfully tweezed and reshaped. Then a facial with soothing creams and astringent herbs. A manicure, a pedicure, and on and on. She was pushed this way and that. A dressmaker came in to measure her and take her sizes. The couturier who had been consigned exclusively to Rayven Cosmetics clicked his tongue and made disapproving noises as each inch of her was noted on his pad. And once he had actually had the audacity to step over and pinch the flesh at the back of her arms. "This must go!" he had scolded. "Kevin Germaine creations are conceived to enhance the body— not to cover fat!"

Caren blushed vividly. She had never considered herself "fat." Not by any measure. "Young lady, you must lose one complete dress size. At least eight pounds. Until then, there is nothing I can do and I shall inform Mr. Rayven as much."

Caren's blush deepened and changed from shyness to humiliation to know that Marc Rayven would be told she was "too fat." Her defenses rising, she turned on the slim, silver-haired Mr. Germaine. "I am not fat! I wear a perfect size ten, and if that's not good enough for you or for Mr. Rayven, that's too bad!"

Immediately, Kevin Germaine's attitude changed to one of grudging respect. "No, no, Miss Ainsley. It's only that if you were to be just a few pounds thinner it would be so much more flattering to you. Please, forgive me if I spoke out of turn—"

A bell sounded and three young girls in pink smocks glided over to Caren and handed her a plate with assorted raw vegetables and a cup of herbal tea. "Miss Ainsley, why don't you go into the office and stretch out? There's no one to bother you and you can rest up from this morning's ordeal. We won't be back to hassle you until around two o'clock," one of the girls offered.

Caren sighed. It sounded too good to be true. A whole hour and a half to just nibble on the rabbit food and stretch out. No poking, no prodding, no snipping or brushing. She was exhausted, she admitted to herself.

It was an elegant, sumptuous office by any standards. Bright green carpeting swirled around Caren's slim ankles; she felt as though she were tripping through a summer meadow. All she needed to complete the feeling was a sprinkling of wild daisies and a few butterflies.

She had never known there were so many shades of green. All in all, it was one of the most restful rooms Caren had ever seen. Light filtered through pale, wheat-colored draperies and the furniture was antique white in French Provincial styling. Long, deep divans lined the walls and pastel-tinted watercolors brought out the light greens of the furnishings. Whoever belongs in this particular office must have a great deal of trouble concentrating on work, she thought. It is so reminiscent of the great outdoors or of city parks in the summer.

Caren walked around the restful office touching one object after another. She was just admiring what appeared to be an intricate telephone system when she heard Marc Rayven's voice. Startled, she whirled around to see if he had just entered the room. He hadn't. His voice was coming over the contraption that passed for a telephone. Caren's face wrinkled into a frown—a definite no-no, according to the makeup specialists in the salon. Besides, when one eavesdropped one never heard anything good about oneself. She should turn the machine off, but how? Most machines had an off button somewhere. Not this machine. Twelve buttons with initials over them. What if she pressed one and Rayven's voice sounded all over the building? A horrible thought struck her. Was this the president's office? Was this sea-green meadow Marc Rayven's office? She shouldn't listen to what was being said, but she wanted to know. Any self-respecting, red-blooded female—and

she was one—would want to know what Marc
Rayven was saying.

Jacques Duval's faint French accent was min-
imal as he spoke quickly, almost too quickly,
Caren thought. "You're sure, Mr. Rayven, that
you want me to follow Ms. Evans' orders exactly?" Was there a touch of defiance in the
Frenchman's tone or was it Caren's imagination?

Marc Rayven's voice purred dangerously over
the wire. "Exactly, Jacques. How is the transformation coming along? Are you molding the
raw material into a length of silk?" Not waiting
for a reply, Rayven continued. "Jacques, I'm
staking my reputation and my company on this
line of cosmetics. No mistakes, no errors of any
kind. You're to follow Moira's instructions to
the letter. I know it's a kind of sow's-ear-silk-
purse thing, but I have the utmost faith in your
ability. That's one of the reasons you're the head
of the salons. By the way, just out of curiosity,
how is our girl taking to this experiment. She is
cooperating, isn't she?"

Sow's ear! Experiment! He thought of her as
"raw material." Well, Mr. Rayven, just you
wait till you see the finished product, she
thought an- grily. Jacques' voice continued to

flow. "Miss Ainsley is very cooperative. I can't say I would do the same if I were in her position. I'm following Ms. Evans' orders to the letter. I certainly hope the both of you know what you're doing. You know, Mr. Rayven, it's times like these that I think I should be selling used cars. I just might do that one of these days."

"Duval, you're talking in riddles. If that's a hint for a raise, why don't you just come out and ask for one instead of telling me you want to sell used cars."

"I don't want a raise. Selling used cars is at least an honest business. When a customer comes in, he knows the chances are ninety to ten that he's going to get a lemon. Here the girl goes to the slau— Never mind. Look, Mr. Rayven, if that's all, I have to get back to the hair salon and work on Denise. She's modeling at three and clients don't wait for Jacques Duval."

"Look, Duval, if something is bothering you, why don't we have a drink after work and talk it out. I'll bring Moira along and we'll discuss it."

"You talk to Moira, Mr. Rayven. I talked to her this morning, and it was enough to last me for the rest of my life. I'm doing my job and that's all that matters or should matter to either of you.''

Caren perched herself on the end of a forest-green chaise and stared at the silent box on the desk. Neither Marc Rayven nor Jacques Duval had said good-bye.

Outrage and anger ripped through Caren at what she considered total disregard for her feelings. She wasn't a piece of merchandise; nor was she a convenience item. Something was going on. Her pulses hammered at the thought that whatever that something was, it boded ill for her. Moira seemed, according to Duval, to be behind whatever it was, but with full authority from Marc Rayven. What was going on? It must have something to do with the new Nightstar line of cosmetics; and if that was true, then it was going to affect her in some way. Sow's ear, raw material! Of all the colossal nerve! and she had gone into the same revolving door with him. Him! Harrumph!

Caren literally flopped down on a grass-green recliner and toppled the raw vegetables onto the floor. The stalks of celery were barely noticeable on the green carpeting. The carrots made a vivid splash of color to Caren's eyes. She ignored both as she sipped at the cold herbal tea. This whole thing was a mistake—a mistake that it was too late to correct.

Caren's back stiffened and her shoulders squared. Whatever was going on, whatever Moira had planned for her, she would fight. She was going to be the best Nightstar girl that Rayven Cosmetics could want. If the stunning Moira was really jealous of her, as Caren suspected, that was her problem. I'll handle my own problems in my own way as they come up. Sow's ear, huh? She would show *him* and Moira Evans as well. From this moment on she was going to be Grade-A silk all the way.

Three

"**Y**ou must be exhausted," Jacques Duval said quietly. To Caren's ears it sounded more like a statement of fact than a question that required an answer. "You're a pleasure to work with," Jacques complimented. "So still and uncomplaining, and with excellent bone structure, I might add." His faint French accent was a pleasure to her ears, and he smiled at her into the mirror in front of which she was sitting.

With a snap of his fingers he summoned a young woman in a pink smock. Murmuring something in French, he gave the girl instructions. In turn, the young woman picked up a brush from the nearby vanity and began to brush Caren's brown hair back off her face into a severe, sleek chignon.

"Oh, Jacques," Caren said hesitantly, "I don't think this style is right for me—"

"*Non, non, chérie*...it is only for the photographs. Soon, we will decide on the proper haircut and style... For now it is only for the photographs.''

"Oh, I see," Caren said quietly. Did he or didn't he like her? Jacques seemed to go out of his way to be polite, but that was it. He made little small talk and he stared at her when he thought she wasn't looking. All in all, Caren was uneasy in his presence. The overheard words on the telephone system rocketed around in her brain, making her frown.

"Never frown. Do you want the number eleven engraved on your forehead?" Jacques demanded suddenly.

Caren apologized. "I guess I was thinking of something and—"

"You don't have to explain, Caren," he replied shortly. Then he repeated something in French to the girl who had just finished her hair. Picking up a soft, flat brush, Jacques dusted Caren's face with the specially blended face powder he had mixed for her that morning. "Now, Caren, if you will come with us, we will take you to the photographer."

Gulping, Caren did as she was instructed, pulling at the ties of the soft gray wrapper that she had been instructed to wear. On her feet were soft, flat-heeled slippers, and she felt decidedly undressed having nothing on beneath the wrapper except her panties.

Obediently, she followed Jacques, who was carrying a tray of makeup, down the hall to a dim little room containing all manner of lights and reflectors that varied from something resembling little umbrellas to sophisticated photographic equipment.

The girl who had brushed her hair back was following behind, brush in hand, and Jacques told her to close the door behind her. From out of the depths of darkness came a voice. "Jacques? Have you brought our little Miss Nightstar?" The owner of the voice stepped into the light.

"Caren, I would like you to meet Bill Valenti, our house photographer," Jacques introduced them.

Bill Valenti was a young man dressed in ragged jeans and, of all things, saddle shoes. His pale face revealed young features and light blond hair that fell onto his shoulders. "How are you holding up, Caren?" the man asked. His friendly manner set Caren at her ease.

"I'm hanging in there, Mr. Valenti." She smiled.

"Bill," he corrected. "Please call me Bill, OK?"

"OK," she said, relaxing still further. There was no threat in his manner, none of Jacques' imperiousness.

Leading Caren over to the platform and into the lights, Bill assured her, "Now, Caren, I want you to relax. I don't want you to stiffen up or worry about how these photos will come out. They're only for our use. For Jacques to study to decide on the perfect hairstyle for you and, of course, your makeup. I want you to think of the camera as your friend. And it is."

Caren looked around her at the frightening equipment, at the glaring lights, and was not comforted by his words. Like most women, she felt the camera lens was a critical viewer, ready and able to pick out each and every flaw and to reveal them to the world.

"You're a very pretty girl, Caren. The camera will see that. And if you think of my lenses as friends, they will be kind to you. Do you think you can do that?" he asked kindly.

Caren gulped and nodded her head. "I'll try, Mr. Val—Bill."

"Good." He smiled boyishly, his eyes meeting hers for the first time. "Good heavens, I

wish we were filming in color. Those eyes! Remarkable! They're going to be a challenge—"
He broke off in midsentence and clapped his hands. "All right, everyone, clear the room. Miss Ainsley and my lenses need some time to form a friendship."

From out of the shadows several people stepped forward and headed for the door. Caren blanched; she had had no idea there had been so many eyes behind those cameras.

"Jacques, you may stay of course. Everyone else, clear the set."

Feeling like a butterfly at the end of a pin, Caren perched on the high stool, aware of her near nakedness beneath the thin gray wrapper. The lights were so bright she felt they would penetrate the soft material and reveal her.

"Now, Caren, I want you to watch what I'm doing with the lights. I want you to see everything; nothing must be a mystery. You will come to know each key light by name; each reflector will become your counterpart. There is no mystery to photography, and once you learn that, the film will capture the woman inside you, Caren. A warm and lovely woman—"

Each word Bill Valenti spoke relaxed Caren still further until she was able to take an interest in the adjustments he was making with the equipment.

"Now, as I was telling you, this is black-and-white film. My intention is to reveal the light-catching surfaces of your face and, of course, those hollows and curves that create shadows. On film your face will become two dimensional, not three. We'll be able to judge your best side, your best features—and, of course, those that we must play down."

Caren frowned.

"Smile, Caren. Even the most beautiful models in the magazines have some feature that is less than flattering in two dimensions. But I'll tell you their secret. They become friends of the camera. They form a relationship; you might even say they have a love affair."

All the while Bill Valenti was talking, Caren could hear the whir and snap of the automatic shutter, the eye that would judge her. But she was so engrossed with what Bill was saying, the little stories, the gossip he was revealing about well-known personalities he had photographed, that she simply forgot the discriminating eye of the camera.

"That's great, Caren. Now, we want to see what that glorious long neck of yours looks like through the lens. Would you open your wrapper, please.''

Caren flushed, flustered. She couldn't; she wouldn't. She would never, never…

"Caren, don't be a silly little girl; Bill only wants you to drop the wrapper off your shoulders,'' Jacques voice reassured.

Feeling like a foolish child, Caren loosened the neck of the gray wrapper, dropping it over her shoulders, her hands clutching the material together over her breasts.

"That's perfect, Caren. Perfect. Now, look this way. That's right, right into the camera. It's your friend, remember?''

Obediently, Caren gazed into the camera, hearing the whirring and the snap of the shutters. Again and again Bill snapped her image, capturing her first from one angle and then from another. All the while his voice soothed her, encouraged her.

Bill Valenti murmured something to Jacques who hurried over to dust Caren's face with powder to remove the shine. She felt as though she were melting, dissolving beneath the glaring lights. But somehow, they warmed her too, filling her with their radiance. Her back was to the camera; she was glancing over her shoulder, her eyes downcast as per Bill's instructions. She thought she heard a sound behind her, but was unable to see.

"That's right, Caren, look down. We want to get a profile shot. OK, now drop your wrapper a little further, that's right—"

Suddenly, a hand touched her, roughly pulling her wrapper up to her shoulders, covering her. A deep, recognizable voice thundered, "What the hell do you think you're doing? The both of you?" Marc Rayven's tone was murderous, causing the blood to curdle in her veins.

"Caren, cover yourself up," he ordered, pulling the wrapper up still further.

Caren was almost afraid to turn around, to see his face. From his tone she knew it must be black with rage, his eyes spewing fire.

"Listen, Valenti, I sent this girl in to you to get preliminary photos, not for a centerfold layout!"

Stammering with confusion, Bill Valenti protested. "Since when is a bare shoulder a 'centerfold layout,'" he demanded. "I don't tell you how to run your business, so don't tell me how to run mine!"

"And you, Jacques, I placed Caren in your hands," Rayven continued, ignoring Bill's statement. The rage in his voice vibrated through the room, bouncing off the walls and coming to rest somewhere near the top of Caren's head. She hated this feeling that she was the cause of the argument, the reason for the man's pounding anger.

So it was that she was startled by the sudden gentleness of his tone when he spoke to her. "Caren, I want you to go back down the hall and get changed. You're through for the day."

Unable to lift her eyes to his, Caren scooted off the stool and headed for the door, before Marc Rayven could resume his tirade. But she wasn't quick enough. His voice thundered again.

"What the hell do you mean by pulling a stunt like that, Bill? Haven't you any decency?"

"What's gotten into you Marc? Since when did you become a prude? You never took on this way with any of the models, and you know as well as I that there was a lot more skin showing than just a bare shoulder and back—"

Something inside of Caren bristled and became rigid, stiffening her spine and freezing her feet to the floor. Pulling the wrapper around her and tightening its belt, she whirled around to face Marc Rayven.

"Stop it this instant!" she demanded hotly

causing the three men to stop and stare at her in amazement. "You can just stop it!" Her eyes were burning through Marc Rayven, incriminating him. "I am not a child, Mr. Rayven, and I certainly have a very high standard of decency. I can assure you that I was not offended or asked to do anything that would compromise that decency. Mr. Valenti and Mr. Duval have been perfect gentlemen. I am not such a babe in the woods that I need Victorian protection from you, and I am affronted that you would think I want to be the Nightstar girl so badly that I would do anything I would be ashamed of." Caren's face burned. Had that been her voice shouting? Had she really said those things to Mr. Rayven? She could feel Bill's and Jacques' glances bouncing back and forth between her and Marc Rayven.

"What did I tell you, Marc?" Bill asked. "Even Caren thinks you're making a fool of yourself. What's gotten into you anyway? I've never seen you like this."

Caren glanced at Jacques and wondered at the knowing look on the Frenchman's face.

Marc Rayven stood his ground. "Drop it, Bill. That's a wrap for today. Jacques, take Caren back to Makeup with you." His tone was tightly measured, refusing to give an inch. Suddenly, he turned on his heel and brushed past Caren and out the door, leaving her with the impression of electrically charged air and a vague scent of his cologne.

Down the hall in Makeup Jacques removed the tight rubber band from Caren's hair and ran his fingers over her scalp soothingly. As he worked, his face was screwed up in a frown.

"Jacques, don't frown. Remember the number eleven." She tried to make light conversation.

Jacques was having none of it. "Mr. Rayven acted very strangely before, Caren. Do you know why?" he asked, his eyes meeting hers in the mirror.

"No, I have no idea.... Actually, I'm ashamed of myself for speaking to him the way I did. I know he was only looking out for my welfare—"

"*Non, non, chérie,* it was more than that." Jacques gave a typical Frenchman's shrug. "I want to reassure you that Bill Valenti is a master of photography and he seems to like you, Caren. He would never compromise you." The frown returned again, accompanied by a look of confusion in the man's eyes and a downturn at the corners of his mouth.

Suddenly, Caren wondered if Jacques was trying to tell her that although Bill Valenti would never compromise her, he himself would. Pushing the thought away as being foolish, Caren managed a smile into the mirror.

"I'm leaving now," Jacques told her. "I'm certain you are happy to be done with this place for the day. By the way, Caren, it really is nice working with you compared to some others around here. I mean that as a compliment."

"Thank you, Jacques, you're very kind. I was told you're the best in the business, so I'm just doing what I'm told. I trust you to do whatever is best for me," Caren said simply.

"That's a mistake."

Caren whirled around and was stunned at the miserable look on the Frenchman's face. "What's a mistake?" she asked, her tone puzzled.

"Trusting anyone. Still, you're young. You have much to learn about people, I'm afraid." The silver wings in his dark hair framed his darkly troubled eyes. Even the short clipped beard gracing his chin seemed to droop a little.

Caren frowned again, she couldn't help it. "Jacques, I was talking about trusting *you*. Trusting you to do whatever is best for me in my transformation into the Nightstar girl. You have such an excellent reputation. Why shouldn't I trust you? I don't understand. Did I say something wrong? If so, I'm sorry." She was babbling and she knew it. Why did Jacques look like this? What was wrong with saying she trusted him?

A look of panic settled over the makeup artist's face. Why? Caren wondered. Better to leave it alone. Something was going on; that was obvious. Sooner or later she would find out what it was that was bothering Jacques and she would deal with it at that time. For now, a simple goodnight should close everything for the day. Tomorrow was something else. "I guess I'll see you in the morning then. Good night, Jacques."

"Good night, Caren," Jacques said just as quickly.

With a last glance at Jacques, Caren left the room and started down the long corridor decorated in gay, colorful murals, toward the bank of elevators. Her mind was buzzing with questions. Questions that no one, it seemed, wanted to answer for her.

Yesterday she had been just another girl in the typing pool and then, suddenly, she was picked to take dictation at the board meeting and her whole life had changed.

Yesterday there had been direction to her life. She had had it all planned. She was going to finish her course at the community college and then apply for a better job, preferably right here at Rayven Cosmetics. Now, nothing was the same. Now, she was going to be the Nightstar girl instead of an executive secretary.

Yesterday she had known who her friends were: the girls in the typing pool, several friends she had made at college, and most of all, Maggie Bryant. Now, there was no way of knowing her friends, and Jacques had just told her not to trust anyone.

Her path to the elevators took her past the door to the photographer's studio. Remembering the scene Marc Rayven had created behind that door made her quicken her step. She still couldn't believe she had stood up to him that way. He was wrong, that's all there was to it, she thought hotly. He had practically accused her of compromising her morals and had accused Jacques and Bill Valenti of being unscrupulous. In her soul Caren knew nothing could be further from the truth. It was true that when Bill instructed her to loosen her wrapper she had panicked. But that had only been for a moment, until Jacques explained exactly what Bill wanted. Centerfold layout, indeed! Marc Rayven, you have a dirty mind!

The express elevator stopped and Caren entered the lonely, brightly lit cage and made the descent to the ground floor of the Rayven building. She shuddered at the sight of the revolving door, waiting a full minute till there was no one in sight before she gave a push and sailed out into the soft, evening air. She really didn't want to go home. A walk. Hadn't Marc Rayven said a brisk walk in the morning was a great way to start the day? Well, maybe it worked that way at night too. A brisk walk home to get her adrenaline flowing and she could sit through four hours of inane chatter on the television shows.

As she stepped briskly along Third Avenue, she again thought of Marc Rayven. Only moments ago she had been thinking of him as a dirty-minded man and here she was taking his advice about a walk. Unconsciously, a smile broke out on her face.

Bill Valenti had been startled and amazed at Mr. Rayven's reaction to a little bit of skin. Hadn't he even said that he'd never known the Lipstick King to behave that way before?

Something inside Caren told her that whatever her original reaction had been to Mr. Rayven's stormy behavior, it was provoked by some protective instinct toward her. Inwardly, she knew she forgave him for the scene he had created. Something inside her told her she would forgive Marc Rayven practically anything.

As she walked, head bent against the wind, Caren's thoughts were jumbled as were her emotions. She jammed her hands into her raincoat pocket, intent only on what she was thinking. Marc Rayven was a very handsome man. She was attracted to him. She felt a flush creep up her neck as she imagined what it would feel like to kiss the tall dark-haired man. The word fantastic came to her lips. Just fantastic.

Moira Evans whirled her way into Caren's thoughts as she waited for the red light to turn green. How many times had Marc Rayven been kissed by his assistant? Plenty ... hundreds ... thousands ... Hrumph, Caren snorted inelegantly. She had kissed a few men in her time, too. So what? But they were boys compared to Marc Rayven. This was where a girl mentally separated the boys from the men and grew up a little herself. An image of Marc Rayven's shoulders floated before her. She imagined that they could blot out the world if he bent toward her with the intention of kissing her. A smile tugged at the corners of her lips. Of course, she would have to be sitting down in that particular fantasy.

The light finally changed and she entered the crosswalk with the others who had been waiting to get to the other side of the avenue. Her busy thoughts spiraled once again. And that glorious warm golden skin of his. How would it be to touch—no, caress—those tawny muscles of his on some secluded beach out of sight of prying eyes? Marvelous. The grin tugged again at the corners of her mouth. So far, she had one fantastic and one marvelous to contend with. For the first time in her adult life her emotions were in a turmoil. She had stirred the simmering pot and now it was about to boil. When that happened you turned down the flame and added a lid. Not so easy, she mused as she stopped to peer into a shop window. When she continued onward, she couldn't remember what she had looked at.

Did Marc Rayven really think she was a gawky schoolgirl? A sow's ear? That hurt—wounded actually. While she might not be bleeding, she definitely felt cut to the quick, not to mention humiliated. How was she going to face him the next time she met up with him? She wasn't flashing and beautiful like Moira, but she did have endurance. And most important, she was a survivor.

What bothered her more than anything, she thought to herself as she waited for another light to change from red to green, was that Marc Rayven was using her. Using her for his own personal gain. The cosmetics business, like the garment industry, was a dog-eat-dog business, and in order to survive and make a fortune, everyone expected you to cut other people to ribbons. Emotionally, Caren knew she could not afford Marc Rayven in any way, shape, or form.

Already, after just a few days, she was becoming short tempered, fearful, and jealous—alien emotions to her. And Marc Rayven seemed to be the catalyst. He was responsible for all these new feelings, all these faint stirrings within her. And when he got what he wanted he would discard her like an old tube of lipstick and she would be left an emotional cripple. He used people. He went after what he wanted and he got it regardless of what or how people felt. She was people. How could he be so nice to her on the surface and say she was a sow's ear to Jacques? He and Moira must have a grand time talking about the ugly duckling, she thought morosely. Soon, the ugly duckling was going to be a beautiful swan if things went the way they were supposed to, and then look out, Moira Evans and Marc Rayven!

Caren slowed her pace. She was almost home. Another two blocks and she would climb the three flights to her apartment, make something to eat and watch the early news. Why did she have to be such an introvert? Introverts, with a lot of help, could be extroverts. She made a mental note to work on that starting the following morning.

Her key in the lock, Caren heard the phone ringing shrilly inside. For some reason, she didn't remember the bell being so loud, so demanding. She closed the door, locked it behind her, and then took her time walking over to the end table. She picked up the beige receiver on the seventh ring and said "Hello."

"Caren?" A slight hesitation as Caren's heart fluttered wildly in her breast. "Marc Rayven here." Not bothering to wait for a reply, he continued. "I know this is short notice. Moira was scurrying all over the building trying to find you, but you had already left. I would like it if you could be ready to go to a party this evening. I'll pick you up at nine. You can be ready, can't you?" Again, he didn't wait for a reply. "This is an important event. Some of the best in the business will be there. You could consider this a sort of preview, so to speak."

Red-hot anger shot up Caren's spine. She'd just bet old Moira was scurrying about looking for her. She and Marc Rayven with their hourly reports. If they knew where she was every hour, why couldn't Rayven's right hand find her? Because she wasn't looking, that was why. And now this...this...Lipstick King—the nickname he had earned when he'd launched the line of lip glosses that had made him famous—was telling her he wanted to take her to a preview. She *was* the preview. She was the one who was going to get a good going over. People were going to pass judgment on her. She wasn't ready yet. How could he do this to her? She was tired. Sow's ear!

"Are you saying you want me to go to a preview or that I am the one who is to be previewed?" she asked coldly, her hand trembling on the tightly clutched receiver.

"A little of both." The friendliness was gone, replaced with a cool authority.

"I'm very tired, Mr. Rayven. I just this minute got in the door and I was looking forward to a quiet evening. Perhaps another time.''

The cool tone was now frigid. ''Perhaps you didn't hear me, Miss Ainsley.'' Before it was Caren. ''I said I would pick you up at nine. A suitable dress is being sent by messenger. It should arrive within minutes. Wear it. I took the liberty of getting your address out of the personnel file, so I know where you live. I heartily endorse punctuality.''

A suitable dress! Well, why not? After all, she was considered a sow's ear. Tacky, in plain English. And why not take her address out of the file? After all, he owned the company and did pay her. Rank certainly did have its privileges. Of all the colossal nerve! She should tell him what to do with his dress, and when he arrived in his custom-made car with the French horn, she should simply refuse to answer the door.

''I'm sure you can't be so tired that a refreshing shower wouldn't do wonders for a person,'' the frigid voice said clearly.

Caren's tone matched his. ''Is that the same as taking a brisk walk in the morning?'' Not waiting for a reply, she rushed on before what little outrage she had deserted her. ''At the orientation meeting this morning I was told that an itinerary would be given to me and that I would have ample notice to prepare before any appearances. This evening's preview does not fall into line with your previous instructions. In short, Mr. Rayven, this sow's ear is not ready to go public. The moment I turn into pure silk I am yours to do with as you see fit. Until that time you will have to make other arrangements. Do I make myself clear?''

"Perfectly. I'll pick you up at nine. Be waiting.'' The line was dead.

Caren replaced the phone and stared at it. The dull buzzer sounded a warning that someone was pressing her worn-out bell in the small lobby of the apartment house. She picked up the phone, pressed six, and spoke harshly. "Yes?"

"Abrams Messenger Service. I have a package for a Miss Caren Ainsley. Shall I leave it or bring it up?"

"I really don't care what you do with it," Caren snapped. "Take it back where you got it from."

"Miss, I can't do that. My boss would fire me. If you don't want to come down for it and you don't want me to bring it up, I'll leave it with the super. You can send it back, but do me a favor and use another messenger service. We have a good reputation. We deliver anywhere in the city and that's our motto. How is it going to look?'' the unseen voice whined.

''All right, all right, you can bring it up. Just leave it by my door.'' Again, Caren replaced the receiver and stood staring at it. She was only committed as long as she accepted the dress box in her hand. For all she cared, it could sit outside her door forever.

The phone shrilled a second time. She really would have to get it checked. ''Caren,'' a sweet, syrupy voice all but cooed. It was Moira Evans. Funny how things changed. Now, she was Caren. Several hours ago she couldn't remember her name. ''Darling, I've been trying to call you and track you down for just hours. There is this preview you simply must attend this evening. I realize this is very short notice, but you were…you were just gone. Marc—Mr. Rayven—feels it is imperative that you attend. I do, too, of course. It's just that you were… Wherever did you disappear to? I, for one, think it was very thoughtless of you not to tell anyone you were leaving. But that is neither here nor there,'' the throaty voice continued. ''You must be ready and available at nine sharp. Mr. Rayven will be picking you up on schedule. And, I must warn you, he is punctual. Of course, I will be with him. I detest tardiness myself.''

Caren stuck her tongue out at the phone in a childish gesture. Now what was she to do? She really had no choices, no options. She had to go. Her decision made, she unlocked her apartment door and picked up a snow-white box tied with a vivid purple bow. She hated purple. She imagined Moira wore purple a lot.

Four

The gold-leaf lettering on the snow-white box read "Albert Nipon," and although Mr. Nipon's creations were definitely out of Caren's financial league, she recognized the name of the famous couturier.

Almost reverently, her fingers untied the satin bow and from out of the pale blue tissue paper she withdrew what had to be the loveliest after-six dress she had ever seen. It was white; more than white, pure white. The most pale lavender beading at the neck and sleeves was repeated at the uneven handkerchief hemline. It was exactly right for her; this she knew instinctively. The white would enhance the pale ivory tones of her skin and those beads would pick up the color of her eyes.

Once again, her eyes fell to the box. There was something more. Her fingers touched the finest silk lingerie bordered with wide bands of

Holland lace. It was exactly right to go under the opaque silk dress. Shoes! Scandalous slippers with modest heels, held on to the foot by an ingenious placing of slender straps.

As she shook out the dress and held it up to herself, something slithered down and fell onto her feet. It was yards of a wide self-belt that could be wrapped cummerbund-style around the waist. Caren decided at once that she would forgo the belt and allow the dress to skim lightly over her figure, presenting the lines of the creation without encumbrance.

Lightly, she stepped over to the mirror to see the dress against her face. Ye gods! Her hair! Jacques had cut it and it was freshly shampooed, but that had been the extent of her hairdressing that day. Jacques had been more concerned with her bone structure and skin tones than her hair. He had told her that the next day would decide what would be done with it.

And Moira, Moira had known. She *had* to have known! Hadn't she received hourly reports on Caren's progress? Marc Rayven was a man; he wouldn't give consideration to the fact that her hair was hanging in dull brown hanks. But Moira would and she would want Caren to embarrass herself.

Quickly, Caren went into the tiny bathroom and surveyed her face, scrutinizing it. Her makeup was still perfect, still bearing Jacques' master hand. But her hair!

It had been cut to a shorter length than she was accustomed to wearing and would be difficult to manage. She just knew that her blow dryer and curling iron would help matters only slightly. It would be possible to take a bath so her makeup wouldn't be ruined, and her fingers and toes were freshly manicured; but what about her hair?

Caren's eyes fell on the kitchen clock. Less than an hour to get ready. Another of Moira's ideas, she was sure. But then again, if she hadn't dawdled on the way home, she would have given herself more time.

No sense crying over it. She had to think of something.

Caren experimented, pushing her hair this way and that, finding each attempt most disappointing. In a flurry of panic she raced out once again to the living room.

Her shaking fingers grabbed up the wide belt. Crossing her fingers for luck, she shook her hair back from her face and began wrapping the belt around her head. Frowning, she examined her attempt and then brightened. The tiny glass beads along the edge of the belt fell flatteringly along her hairline, softening its severity and accentuating her features and Jacques' masterful makeup artistry. She had never attempted anything so sophisticated before and felt a little self-conscious. But she reminded herself that she was the Nightstar girl and sophistication and style would be required of her.

Feeling much more self-assured, she hurried once again to the bathroom and ran the tub, making certain to leave the door open so the tiny room wouldn't fill with steam and cause her makeup to streak.

Forty minutes later Caren was dressed. The silk slip felt cool and luxurious against her skin. The dress was perfect, no doubt altered according to the measurements that had been taken of her earlier that day. Even the shoes felt as though they had come from her own wardrobe and fitted perfectly.

Her concern was centered on the head covering she had designed. Turning her head this way and that, she began to feel more confident about it. The belt had been yards long, meant, no doubt, to be wrapped several times around the waist and then to fall in long ends to the hemline. Instead, she had centered it across her forehead and crisscrossed it in the back, bringing it up over the top of her head and crisscrossing it again, repeating this several times until her entire head was covered. Finally, taking both long ends, she fashioned them into a soft knot resembling a rosette. This she secured over her right ear with pins. The resulting effect was sophisticated and exotic, the little drooping beads falling symmetrically across her brow and tickling her pleasingly.

Suddenly, the doorbell buzzed. A quick glance at the clock. Fifteen minutes early! Wasn't that just like Moira? Hoping to catch her at a disadvantage in front of Marc Rayven. Smiling to herself, Caren picked up her house key and slipped out of her apartment. She would meet them downstairs and save herself reason for apologizing for her small, sparsely furnished apartment. As she closed the door behind her, she once again heard the impatient buzzing of the bell. Darn that Moira!

Flouncing down the three flights to the door, Caren's feet felt as though she were walking on air. She looked stunning and she knew it. She was going to stand up straight and keep her chin up. Mr. Nipon's dress wasn't going to be wasted on a bumbling little schoolgirl. She was a woman and she looked her best, better than she had ever looked, and she was going to show the world she was aware of it.

When she opened the door of the vestibule, it was not Moira Evans' finger pressed impatiently on the buzzer to her apartment; it was that of Marc Rayven himself. When he turned at her entrance, she could have sworn she saw his jaw drop. The appreciative look in his eyes gave her further confidence and she preened. A sow's ear, was she!

"Mr. Rayven, how nice of you to come early," she said, with just a touch of sarcasm in her tone.

"Actually, Miss Ainsley," said Moira Evans stepping out from the other side of the vestibule, "we arrived early in case you needed any help dressing."

"Yes, Caren. That was Moira's helpful suggestion," Marc interjected. "But as you can see, Moira, Caren is perfect—just perfect."

Caren felt Moira glaring at her. It was evident to her that the woman was hoping to catch Caren with her hair down and rushing around like a madwoman trying to get her act together. Alien and dangerous feelings rose in Caren as she smiled sweetly at Moira, taking pleasure from the stiff set of her shoulders. "How nice of you to think of me, Miss Evans. But as you can see, I did the best I could all by myself. I haven't needed anyone to wait on me since I was a little girl." She felt her smile broaden and her words were sugary sweet. Moira had attacked her self-respect by indicating that Caren was incapable of making herself presentable enough to be seen in public.

Marc seemed oblivious to the hostility between the two women as he opened the outside door to usher them out. Men, Caren thought hotly. World War III could be going on right under their noses and they wouldn't notice it. They all thought their own sex had a monopoly on doing battle. When would they realize that it really was the female of the species who was deadlier than the male?

It was Caren's arm that Marc tucked under his own as they went down the front stairs, leaving Moira on her own to teeter on her incredibly high heels. It was Caren who was helped into the front seat of Rayven's Mercedes, leaving Moira to struggle into the back seat. It was at this point that Caren noticed the shiny black satin of Moira's skin-tight sheath dress. The long tight sleeves and figure-hugging bodice showed her pencil-slim figure to perfection. Against the white of Caren's dress, the black made Moira seem sensual and sexy, almost vampish, an effect that Caren was almost certain Moira had planned.

"We're going to a preview of a new film and all of New York will be there, including photographers and columnists. That's why I felt it was important for you to attend. You understand, there will not be a formal announcement made at this time of our new Nightstar campaign and the part you play in it. It's enough for now for people to wonder who this pretty new face is. Understand?" Marc spoke quietly as he drove, addressing his remarks to Caren and from time to time glancing over at her, a strange new light in his eyes.

"I understand," Caren answered, knowing without being told that anyone new whom Marc Rayven was seen with was automatically newsworthy. "So you don't want me to say anything about Nightstar if I'm asked."

"Right. Just smile that dazzling smile of yours and act mysterious. Think you can handle it? I'll be right there at your side; I'll help fend off some of the more pointed questions," he assured her.

"I understand, Mr. Rayven."

"Marc. You must call me Marc." His hand covered hers, as it rested on her lap, and squeezed it meaningfully, causing Caren's heart to leap to her throat.

Moira, in the back seat, was oblivious to the intimate contact between the two up front and she commented stridently, "Of course, it will be Mr. Rayven at the office, Miss Ainsley. Understood?"

Before Caren could answer, Marc's voice thundered, "I have just told Caren to use my first name and that's the way I want it, Moira. Both at the office and outside the office."

"Marc...I just...well, it's always been your policy not to fraternize with the help, I just thought—"

"Don't think, Moira. And besides, Caren is not 'help.' She's my Nightstar girl." Marc squeezed Caren's hand again.

"Do you think she can handle it tonight? About remaining mysterious, I mean. You know that any woman you're seen with creates a stir. What do they call you—New York's most eligible bachelor? What I mean is, Miss Ainsley doesn't know how to deal with this segment of society—''

"That's enough, Moira," Marc said wearily. "All Caren has to remember is not to say anything about working for Rayven Cosmetics or the Nightstar campaign. You can handle that, can't you, sweetheart?" Sweetheart! Sweetheart! From a sow's ear to sweetheart! Instantly, Caren pulled her hand away, dropping the keys she had quickly grabbed before she had left the apartment. She didn't have an evening bag that would go with Mr. Nipon's creation, so she had thought it better not to take one at all.

"What's this?" Marc asked picking up the jangle of keys from the seat beside him.

"My keys. I...I didn't have a bag to go with the dress—''

"Moira, take a note. I want Caren to have a complete new wardrobe—from soup to nuts. Understand? Nothing but the best."

"But I...really don't need—''

"Nonsense. I've admired the tailored suits and dresses that you've worn to the office, but now it's time for you to be wearing designer labels. OK?"

Of course it was OK! It was especially OK since he had mentioned that he'd noticed her at the office and the clothes she'd worn. It was extra-specially OK since he'd just said he admired her taste.

The keys still jangled in his hand and he slipped them into his tuxedo pocket.

"My keys—"

"I'll keep them for you, Caren." He took his eyes off the road long enough to look over at her and smile that bewitching smile. "I'll give them back when I take you home."

"Home," Moira was heard to mutter from the back seat. It was evident the woman was positively seething. "I'd say that was a pretty questionable neighborhood, if you ask me."

"Oh really?" Marc asked, looking straight ahead at the traffic. "I thought it was all right. It reminded me of the neighborhood where my first apartment was. I was pretty independent when I went to college," he said aside to Caren. "I wanted to try my own wings and leave the family fortune in the bank where it belonged. I took a loft in the Soho district with a couple of friends, and I still think those were the best days of my life. I loved it. All the world seemed to pass right by the front door, and many of the friends I made were artists and writers. Happily, some of them are very famous and successful today. I still count them among my friends.''

Somehow, Caren couldn't quite see Marc Rayven as the ''poor little rich boy'' but something in his tone made her heart go out to him. She was about to ask him about some of his well-known friends when Moira interrupted.

''Oh, Marc, you make it sound so romantic and it wasn't that way at all and you know it! Remember the days when there was little else to eat except canned spaghetti and chicken noodle soup? That wasn't all that much fun.''

Caren's ears perked up. Had Moira known Marc since their college days? That would make her somewhere in her thirties? She was surprised as she had always thought Miss Evans was only a little older than herself. Surprise dissolved away into a curious kind of jealousy that Moira had shared an experience with Marc that was obviously close to his heart. Jealous? No, she denied, it *had* to be something else! How could she be jealous of a man who had called her a sow's ear?

Marc was silent and Moira, suspecting she had said the wrong thing, began to amend her first statement. ''Actually, though, it was rather fun. Marc,'' she said excitedly, ''remember the time your English Lit professor was going to fail you if you didn't pass the exam? And remember how we stayed up all night for three nights helping you cram? And remember how we all waited outside the lecture hall for you to finish your exam, and remember the party we had afterward?''

Marc laughed, a deep booming sound. "Yes, and I also remember how you spent a whole day preparing all my favorite foods and how angry you were when I fell asleep, too tired to eat."

"Ooh, you used to make me so angry!" Moira laughed, a deep, throaty, sensual sound that vibrated through Caren's very being. They talked so intimately, had so many memories to share. A disquieting thought occurred to Caren. From the sound of their conversation, it appeared Marc and Moira had lived together. Again that curious worm of discontent rolled around in her innards. Was it possible they still maintained that relationship and kept it secret from the office? No; she negated the thought. Otherwise, the society columns would link Moira Evans' name with Marc's. Moira wasn't the kind of woman to share her man with another woman. And besides, if their relationship was an intimate one going back over the years, why weren't they married by now? From the signals Moira was sending, Marc's continuing bachelorhood was definitely not her preference. So it had to be Marc who wasn't serious about Moira. The little worm of discontent stilled and a pervasive sense of well-being took its place.

Coming out from the dark theater into the bright lights of the lobby, Caren felt blinded. The film was being soundly acclaimed as a work of genius; voices echoed its praise all around her. Caren sighed. Perhaps there was something wrong with her, but she hadn't been able to follow the film. Its meaning was all a mystery to her. She supposed she was behind the times, but she still preferred the sharp wit of a Tracy and Hepburn film or the schmaltzy melodrama of a romance between Clark Gable and Lana Turner. Even those old Charlie Chan movies gave her more pleasure.

Moira was speaking to several people and uttering words like "divine" and "inspired." A hand took Caren by the arm and led her away from the milling crowd exiting the theater. All around her were the scions of society; it was rumored that Jacqueline Onassis was somewhere in the throng. Marc's voice sounded alarmingly close to her ear. ''Remember what we discussed in the car. And yes, you loved the film.''

''Look this way, Mr. Rayven!'' a voice from the perimeter of the crowd called. Both Caren and Marc looked in the direction of the voice as flashbulbs exploded.

''Marc! How nice to see you again!'' a woman in a stunning creation of rainbow silk called out. In her hands she carried a miniature tape recorder, the trademark of Cassandra Phillips. The woman's shrewd eyes slid over Caren speculatively, but to Caren's credit, she lifted her chin and met the woman's challenging gaze, a sweet smile stretching her lips.

''Cassandra. I should have known you would be here.'' Marc grinned. ''No preview is complete without you and your recorder. I suppose you want to know what I thought of the film?'' he asked looking at the small recorder she carried in the palm of her hand.

Caren recognized the name Cassandra and knew that this was *the* Cassandra Phillips, the society columnist for the *Daily Journal.* The woman beamed at Marc and then transferred her pointed gaze to Caren. Imperceptibly, Marc's controlling hand on her arm pushed Caren into the foreground. He had instinctively known the columnist was not interested in his critique of the film; her curiosity was centered on the beautiful creature on his arm.

"Never mind the film, Marc." Cassandra smiled. "Everyone knows it will be a raging success." Still her eyes had not left Caren. "Are you going to be rude, Marc, which is so unlike you, or are you going to introduce me to this charming young lady?"

"Of course, Cassandra, may I present Caren Ainsley."

"Ainsley. Of the Newport Ainsleys? No? My dear, you're positively ravishing. Without turning around I can tell you that every male eye in the room is on you."

Caren flushed and murmured a response to the compliment.

"Marc, where did you find this enticing beauty? Tell me, my readers will be delirious at the new face in tomorrow's early edition. Would you mind if I borrowed Miss Ainsley for a few moments to get some pictures?"

"Not at all; I'm sure Caren would be delighted."

Cassandra turned to Caren. Her eyes clearly recognized the designer dress. "Nipon creations photograph well." It was Caren's turn to smile.

Cassandra stared a moment longer at Caren as though she couldn't quite make up her mind about something. "Marc, do you mind if I introduce Miss Ainsley around? Instead of single I think I'd rather have group shots. My readers will think it more exciting. Perhaps one or two of you together, but I can't promise that you'll see them in print."

"You're the expert, Cassandra," Marc said gallantly.

Cassandra steered Caren toward a group of people on the other side of the room.

From that point on, everything became a blur. She was meeting people whose names she had read in the newspapers and magazines—news correspondents, actors, actresses, television personalities.... They all asked her many questions, some pointedly inquiring as to her background, where she worked, what her plans were. Deftly, she avoided giving direct answers to their questions, hedging where she could, but mostly giving short answers and turning the conversation around to ask them about their own lives and work. All the while Cassandra stood nearby, her palm holding the miniature recorder extended. Flashbulbs popped and cameras clicked continuously.

Miraculously, her maneuvers worked. The best way to talk to someone was to talk about *them*, not herself. From Cassandra's approving glance it was clear that Caren was a success.

Marc, with Moira in tow, rescued her from the crowd. She was aware that her picture was being snapped constantly, but it wasn't until several reporters, pen in hand, broke through to her and demanded, "Miss Ainsley, how does it feel to be Marc Rayven's new Nightstar girl?" that she felt the blood drain from her face. How had they found out? Who? How?

From the black looks Marc was bestowing on her it was clear he believed she had spilled the beans. But she hadn't!

A frown of displeasure settled on Cassandra's face. Her shrewd gaze traveled swiftly to Marc Rayven. Instantly her hand-held recorder was placed in front of Marc as the reporter demanded, "How long did you think you could keep this secret, Mr. Rayven? Is Nightstar the name of a new line of cosmetics? Tell us all about it," the reporter pleaded. "What can the women of the world expect from Rayven Cosmetics in the weeks to come?"

"Actually, we were hoping to keep it secret until we formulated our entire campaign—"

Marc began, his eyes piercing Caren's like knife points.

Cassandra turned back to Caren. "My readers will want to know your feelings on the matter, Miss Ainsley. My column could help you immensely." Again her long slender arm shot out, the small cassette held firmly for all to see.

Flabbergasted, Caren glanced wildly around. Her eye fell on Moira who was displaying a forbidding expression. Before she could answer, Marc seized her by the hand and literally dragged her out of the theater and ordered his car to be brought around immediately.

Outside in the brisk night air, she stood beside him, waiting for the Mercedes. Moira, breathless, joined them. "I thought we had it all clear, Miss Ainsley. You were not to say anything about—"

"But, Marc, I didn't! I swear—"

"It seems as though your little Miss Ainsley couldn't wait for her fame and she spilled the beans. I hope you don't think you can hold us up for more money on the Nightstar contract just because your face will be splashed over every newspaper in New York!" Moira threatened the astonished Caren. "Just remember, you're nothing but an insignificant typist and we can always find someone really deserving of the assignment—''

"That's enough, Moira," Marc stilled his assistant with a deadly calm voice. "Why don't you catch a cab home? I'll take Caren home."

Moira's mouth literally flapped open. Then she resumed her composure and stared at Caren as if to say, "Now you're going to get it!"

When the Mercedes was brought around, Marc helped Caren into the car and hopped behind the wheel. They had driven several blocks before he spoke to her.

"That was a foolish mistake on your part, Caren. I thought I could count on you to follow orders."

"You're not going to believe me, Marc. But I honestly didn't say anything! I have no idea how they found out! I was talking—no, listening, and suddenly those reporters began flashing my picture—"

"I want to believe you. I know you're not sophisticated like those people back there. I know how they can get things out of a person and the word is out before you know it—"

"No, Marc, I definitely did not tell anyone! I'm not a child, even if I'm not ultrasophisticated. I should know whether or not I said anything, and I didn't. Mostly, I was getting them to talk about themselves.''

''They could only have known if you told them! What's done is done and we'll have to go on from here. I don't want to hear another word about it. You've said enough for one night!''

Caren bit her lips, silencing herself. If she were three years old, she would have thrown herself on the floor of the car and kicked and screamed and cried her eyes out! But she wasn't three years old and she had to sit here like a grown-up and take it.

When they were almost back to her apartment, Marc's anger seemed to have dissipated. ''I must say you made quite a conquest in Cassandra Phillips. And she's one tough cookie. She's been around for so long, she can tell a phony just by looking. You handled yourself quite nicely and I'm proud of you. That sector of society can be a sea of sharks when they want to be. But they certainly seemed to like you. Even before they found out about Nightstar—''

''You just passed my house,'' Caren interrupted coldly. ''Stop here and let me out.''

As instructed, Marc pulled over to the curb. The car was still in motion when Caren opened the door and leaped out. Without a backward glance she ran to the brownstone where she lived. The devil take Marc Rayven and the devil take Nightstar. She didn't like being called a liar and that was exactly what he had done!

Blinded by tears, she scaled the high steps to the front door and pushed against it. When she was between the doors in the tiny vestibule, she realized that her key was in Marc's pocket. Damn! Damn! It was late. Her face was streaked with tears! She didn't want to face the superintendent of her building and make all kinds of explanations. Not now. She wanted to hide away from the world, curl up in a ball, and lick her wounds—wounds inflicted by Marc Rayven.

Her knees were shaking so badly they threatened to give out under her weight. Back against the wall, she slid down onto her heels, curling her head to her knees and covering it with her arms. Silent sobs tore at her throat. I won't cry! I won't cry! she scolded herself.

The door had opened so silently that she hadn't heard it. Suddenly, strong hands were pulling her to her feet and gathering her into waiting arms. Marc pressed her face to his broad chest and soothed her with small, tender caresses.

"Caren," he whispered, "I came to bring you your key. I didn't mean to make you cry—"

"I'm not crying! I...I'm just...tired."

"I'm a beast. Tell me, tell me what a beast I am," his voice was soft, softer than she'd ever heard any man's voice. His hand cupped her chin, lifting her face. "I'm sorry, Caren. Say you forgive me," he whispered; then his mouth covered her own.

Her protests were only momentary. She felt herself go limp in his strong embrace. Hungry lips pressed on hers and her confusion welled as he pulled her closer and closer into his powerful embrace. Imperceptibly, his lips became more demanding and his hands molded themselves down her spine, pressing her into his lean, hard body—his body that was as unyielding as steel.

Disconnected thoughts of running, seeking shelter, finding safety from this man assaulted her. But he was creating a dizziness in her head, fogging her thoughts, robbing her of any will, save his own. And he willed her to respond, demanded it.

His kiss became gentle, tender, his lips clinging to hers. Their breaths mingled and Caren felt herself become warm and supple against him. Against her own will, her senses reeled and soared, making her dizzy, making her want more; she pressed herself closer, always closer.

A riot of emotions whirled through her; seizing her in their grip and arousing in her wants and desires she had never known. The dark, tiny vestibule became the top of the world and she spun and turned in an orbit of Marc Rayven's making. The cracked and painted ceiling became the dome of the heavens, its nightstars gleaming brightly against the velvet black of the universe. And when her knees threatened to buckle beneath her, his arms held her, supporting her, taking her with him on a flight to the moon where desire would be fed by passions. Caren became a willing passenger; her ticket was stamped "One Way" and that was up, up, up. A need ignited within her, a need she had never known she possessed. She wanted Marc Rayven. She wanted his touch, his caress, his kiss. And when his lips upon hers hinted at unexplored heights of passion, she wanted to chart those realms with him.

Her arms wrapped around his neck, her fingers grazed through the thick, curling hair at the back of his head. She could feel the sheer strength of his body against hers, could sense the needs rising within him. In spite of herself, because of herself, she wanted to answer those needs.

Roughly, Marc put her away from him. Confused, she gazed up into his face, unable to read the spectrum of emotions she saw there. Suddenly, the night air felt cold upon her cheek. A faint sense of abandonment and desolation fell over her like a gossamer veil. Unable to speak, too stunned by his sudden unexplained reaction, she could only look at him questioningly.

"I didn't mean to do that. It was only when I came in here and found you crying—"

"I wasn't crying.... Why, why did you do that?" she insisted, her voice a harsh whisper.

"Why did I kiss you?" he asked, his familiar insolence and arrogance returning.

"I should slap you, kick you, do something. You had no right to call me a liar! You had no right to kiss me that way!" Her instinctive self-preservation was returning. But it felt empty and hollow compared to the feelings he had aroused in her.

Marc Rayven's face hardened into lines carved from granite. He picked up her hand and dropped her keys into it. "I kissed you, Miss Ainsley, because I wanted to see if your mouth was as good for loving as it is for telling company secrets.''

Without another word, he turned on his heel and left the tiny vestibule where he had given Caren a glimpse of the heights and depths her passions could reach. He left her alone, confused, and angry. She could deal with those emotions, she told herself as she let herself into the apartment building. What she couldn't deal with was the humiliation she had suffered since coming to know that...that...Lipstick King— Marc Rayven.

Five

Caren sat quietly, allowing Jacques to work on a new shade of makeup blended especially for her. The Frenchman seemed as preoccupied as she herself was. From time to time she watched him as he risked a glance in her direction out of the corner of his eye.

She still hadn't recovered from the night before. Marc's effect on her consciousness was almost tangible and she found herself looking endlessly into the mirror to see if the imprint of his mouth was still on her lips. Last night had opened her eyes in more ways than one. First, she now felt confident that she could hold her own in the upper crust, Marc Rayven's social stratum, the echelon that being the Nightstar girl would thrust her up to.

Secondly, she knew there was a traitor in their midst. And more likely than not, that traitor had been wearing a skin-tight black satin Givenchy.

And last, but not least, she learned that Marc Rayven could transport her into worlds she had never known existed.

Caren admitted to herself that she did have a competitive spirit. She didn't like being made a fool of by Moira Evans, and she was determined to do something about it. She was also determined to throw herself into this Nightstar business and make the best darn Nightstar girl Marc Rayven could ever want. She would prove Moira wrong if it was the last thing she did on this cold, cold earth.

"What do you think of this shade of mulberry for your eyes?" Jacques asked, making her blink and come away from her thoughts.

Caren shrugged. "You're the expert. What do you think?"

"Just a little lighter," he said, turning his back on her and deftly adding a smidgen of white powder to his pot of feathery dust.

Caren remembered Moira's proprietorial air concerning Marc—her attempts to malign Caren in Marc's eyes. Not that she had needed to do much, Caren decided, remembering his remark about a sow's ear. It was clear to her that Marc had been trying to prove a point to the members of the board when he'd chosen her to be the

Nightstar girl. And since making that foolhardy decision on the spur of the moment, he now found himself stuck with it.

Still, hadn't he told her last night that he had noticed her and admired her style of clothing? Don't be a silly, she told herself. That was just her old competitive spirit rising again, trying to give her confidence. But someday, she promised, someday she would make Marc Rayven eat those words about a sow's ear.

As she watched Jacques, Caren thought of the expression on Moira's face when Marc had suggested she take a cab home and that he would take Caren home. Sheer hatred, deep and pure, had been written on her features. Any ninny could have seen it—and Caren was no ninny.

"I think we're ready to try this out now," Jacques said with brush poised in midair.

Caren leaned back in the velour chair, much the way she would have done had she been at the dentist's. She felt rather than saw Jacques stiffen at Moira's words.

"You *do* want to darken that mulberry shade, don't you, Jacques? We want this little pigeon to be perfect now, don't we?" Moira said sarcastically.

Now, where had she come from? Caren

moaned inwardly. Why couldn't Marc's assistant wait until the end of the hour to check on things? Every time the black-haired, sleek-figured woman was within ten feet of her she felt as though she were trapped in a fishnet and would never get free.

Caren opened her eyes. Jacques had indeed stiffened. As a matter of fact, he was positively rigid and Caren, from her position in her sky-blue chair, could see his normally firm hand tremble a little.

"Impossible! This particular shade of mulberry wasn't meant for someone of Caren's coloring. Any fool with an ounce of sense could tell you that!" Caren had never heard Jacques' voice so angry, so enraged. He had spoken through tight lips, barely controlling himself.

It was Moira's turn to grow rigid. Her voice was the stab of an icicle when she replied. "Are you insinuating I'm a fool?" Not waiting for a reply, she continued. "Because if you are, you can pick up your salary at the cashier."

Caren thought the Frenchman was going to ignore Moira's comment as he bent over to brush the soft powder against her eyelid. Instead, he brushed lightly and then turned, his movements perfectly controlled. "*Marc Rayven* hired me and *Marc Rayven* will have to fire me. However, that is neither here nor there at this moment. I just might take you up on my resignation. But,'' and his voice suddenly hardened, "not before I transform this young woman into the Nightstar girl. Don't tempt me, Moira, because you might come to regret it. Do we understand each other?''

Moira's face flushed to the same shade Jacques was holding in his hand. For a split second Caren noticed that Moira Evans was actually a very ugly woman with her face contorted in rage. However, Moira recovered quickly and with a last angry look at Jacques, she stalked from the room, her spike heels tapping on the tile floor.

Now, what was *that* all about? Caren wondered as she leaned back against the chair. She was disappointed when Jacques offered no explanation for the scene she had just witnessed.

Ugly duckling, sow's ear. The words kept ricocheting around in Caren's brain as she remained dutifully still while Jacques worked on just the right shading and toning for her skin. Twice he wiped the mulberry shadow from her eyes till he had what he called perfect shading.

Caren felt herself slipping into a light sleep

and gave a small start. "I'm sorry," she apologized.

"No problem," Jacques said, moving back a few feet. He stared at Caren from first one angle and then another. "I think we're going to see a big difference in this batch of photographs. Yesterday was a sort of trial-and-error session. Rayven will be pleased, you have my word." His tone was impersonal and cool and it surprised Caren.

"I didn't see the pictures yesterday. Neither Mr. Rayven nor Moira said anything last evening to me about them. How bad were they?" Caren asked fearfully, imagining the worst,

"Bad," the makeup artist said curtly. "It was my fault. I was off my feed yesterday, and any session with Moira Evans automatically makes me do my worst. For whatever good it is, you have my apologies."

"Accepted." Caren grinned.

Jacques merely nodded. "Rayven is going to be in the studio when they photograph you. I'm not sure about Moira. Can you handle working with the boss watching?"

"I don't know," Caren said honestly. How was she to act when she looked at him and remembered the feel of his arms and his lips? And if Moira was there, it would be worse.

Jacques shrugged again. "Rayven is a nice guy. As a matter of fact, he's one hell of a guy. He's fair. Always remember that." Suddenly, his tone softened. "You must think this place is weird, and I can't say that I blame you. Trust me. You really can, you know. Just do your job and go home. That's the best advice I can give you at the moment. Don't allow yourself to become involved with the inner workings of this company. If you should, for some reason, suddenly find that you have a problem, or something comes up that you feel threatens your position as the Nightstar girl, go to Rayven. And remember, he's fair. He'll listen."

Caren was stunned by Jacques' words. Was he trying to warn her about something and taking the long way around in telling her? Why couldn't people just say what they meant and leave it at that?

Evidently, Jacques was not expecting an answer to his remarks for he had already begun to pack up his pots and brushes and was making notations on the colors and shadings he had used on her. An "OK, thanks for telling me," was all Caren could manage.

"Don't mention it, *chérie*," he said warmly, looking up from his notepad to glance at her in the mirror and smile. "They are expecting you in the hair salon in fifteen minutes. Before you go, there is something I want to try."

Caren nodded and watched as Jacques picked up a skein of hair that was variegated shades of blond. He began to pick through the colors and was holding them up to her face.

"Oh, no, Jacques. I don't think...I don't want to be a blonde!"

"No, no, *chérie*. You are by nature a brunette. *Never* would I suggest anything so drastic, so artificial. But look here. See?" He was holding a hank of hair just shades lighter than her own against her face at the temples and hairline. "See the way the slightly lighter shade enhances those fabulous eyes you have? And see what it does for your skin tones? I was only suggesting a streaking, much the way the sun would lighten your hair. See?"

Caren had to admit that the difference in hair shades was only slight, but the effect was astounding. Now why hadn't she herself ever thought of that? "You're a marvel, Jacques, and I do trust you."

"*Oui, chérie.*" He smiled, making his perfectly manicured mustache lift in humor. "Now, I will call in an assistant to cleanse your face and then I will take you to the hair salon myself. I will put you into the hands of a protégé of mine, Henri. OK?"

"OK," she agreed, liking Jacques more today than she had yesterday.

"Good, I will leave you now, but I will be back in a few minutes." Picking up several implements from his vanity table, he exited the room and Caren could hear him calling for an assistant to attend to her.

A harried-looking girl, carrying a portfolio under her arm, entered the room. Immediately, she began to apply cold cream to Caren's face, removing all traces of Jacques' artwork.

"Couldn't we just leave the makeup? It seems so senseless to have Jacques go to all that trouble to apply it again later."

"Oh no, Miss Ainsley. Mr. Duval has given express orders that you were to have nothing but a moisturizer on your skin when you sit under the dryer. The heat would spoil the makeup anyway and it would also drive impurities into your skin," the chatty assistant explained. "And I also happen to know that Mr. Rayven himself has given Mr. Duval express orders that nothing, absolutely nothing, be allowed to destroy your peaches-and-cream complexion. So many women positively ruin their complexions by improper cleansing—'' The girl continued, but her words were falling on deaf ears.

Caren's thoughts were centered on this new information. Marc Rayven himself had given the order that nothing should destroy her peaches-and-cream complexion? That seemed an overstatement. While she had never had skin problems, she had never considered her complexion peaches and cream. But Marc Rayven had! It would seem he had noticed much more about her than she had ever dreamed. Yet something didn't fit. How could a man who admitted he had noticed her figure and clothes and now, she discovered, her complexion, and had admired those features make a remark about a sow's ear?

"Miss Ainsley...Miss Ainsley?" The girl was pulling Caren away from her musings. "Would you care for a cup of tea before Mr. Duval takes you to the hair salon?"

"Yes, that would be lovely."

"I'll get it for you immediately. I'll be right back."

When the girl had left the room, Caren noticed the portfolio she had brought into the room sitting on the vanity. Spying her name printed on the front piqued her curiosity and she leaned forward and picked it up. The label stated that it contained photos—the photos Bill Valenti had taken of her the day before.

Curiously, Caren opened the portfolio and withdrew the eight-by-ten glossy prints. What she saw almost made her gag! It was her own face, or was it? It was barely recognizable! She looked hard, a painted lady—if ''lady'' could be used in the loosest terms. There were deep shadows over her eyes and in the hollows of her cheeks. Her hair, being sleeked back as it had been, added no softness to the jaded look. Even her lips gleamed darkly in the black-and-white photos, making her appear vampish. She stared at the photos, hardly believing she was looking at herself.

Caren was sick inside. Her innards churned and nearly bolted. She hadn't looked like this when she had walked into the studio; what had Bill Valenti done to her? Maybe there was something wrong with the lighting. Astounded eyes fell on the photos of her bare shoulder, her face tilted down, profile to the camera. Looking up into the mirror, her hand smoothed across her cheeks. There were no deep hollows there; why had the camera picked them up?

Behind her she heard a voice. Jacques Duval. She saw him frown when he saw the pictures opened on her lap.

"Oh, Jacques. This is terrible! This isn't me! I hardly recognize myself. What did Bill Valenti do to me!"

Jacques' shoulders slumped. "It wasn't Bill Valenti, *chérie,* it was me."

"You? But why…how? I didn't look like that when I walked into the studio to have my photos taken!"

"*Oui, chérie.* You did. Only you couldn't see it because you do not see in black and white and the camera did. Even Bill Valenti could not see it through the lens. It was done with varying shades of tints…. No matter how it was done, I, *chérie,* betrayed you." Jacques lowered his head, ashamed.

Caren gasped, astounded by the man's revelation. Suddenly, a thought struck her and she almost cried. "Jacques…last night…at the premier, newspaper photographers—"

"*Non, non, chérie,* that was an original part of the plan, but I couldn't go through with it.

Remember, I touched up your face after the hot lights. I corrected my...my sin.''

"Original part...what plan?''

"Let it go, *chérie*. You were sabotaged, but not today. No, not today!'' he said vociferously, raising his hand and beating on the back of the chair she sat in, his anger making her quake.

"Say you forgive me, *chérie*. Please...I could not go through with it.''

"But who put you up to this?'' A sudden thought occurred to her. Had Marc Rayven, realizing his error in making her the Nightstar girl ordered Jacques...? "Jacques, just tell me, was it Marc Rayven?''

"No! Never! I swear, *chérie*. It was planned so Marc Rayven would think himself a fool to have chosen you—''

"Say no more, Jacques. I'm not a child and I can put two and two together. This is what Moira Evans and you were talking about when I came up to Makeup yesterday, isn't it? And that was why she came in here today, to be certain you were continuing with the plan.''

"*Oui,*'' the Frenchman said sadly. And then raising his head with dignity, he looked her straight in the eye. "But Jacques Duval is not an evil man, *chérie*. Nor will I succumb to threats any longer. As long as I am with Rayven Cosmetics, I will be your slave. I will protect you and give you the best of my talent. Please, *chérie,* forgive a fool.''

Caren's anger abated. He was so contrite, so sincere, he went straight to her heart. Tenderly, she lifted her hand and placed it on Jacques' bowed head. "I forgive you, Jacques; and I need you. Today is another day and we will put this behind us. I only ask one favor. If Mr. Rayven has not seen these photos yet, I would like it if he never sees them.''

"There is no need to protect me, *chérie.* I will throw myself on his mercy—'' In his agitation, Jacques' French accent was becoming more pronounced and he was revealing his Frenchman's penchant for being melodramatic.

"No, I don't want Marc to see these pictures. And as far as protecting someone, I'm not—I promise you. It's just a simple matter of learning the rules, Moira Evans' rules. And knowing the rules is a big part of winning the game." A slow smile spread over her face and soon Jacques was smiling too.

"Mademoiselle is the most generous, most beautiful—''

"No, Jacques." Caren stopped his words with

a raised hand. "The mademoiselle is your friend."

In the hair salon Jacques hovered over her like a mother hen. Each and every hair that Henri wrapped in aluminum foil was inspected by Jacques himself. Henri, another Frenchman, had listened attentively to a long diatribe in his native language, and when he approached Caren it was with profound respect.

Diligently, Henri worked, lifting tiny sections of hair around her hairline and the nape of her neck with the tail of his comb. Much discussion took place between himself and Jacques before Henri applied the foamy bleaching solution to each minuscule section of hair and wrapped each in strips of foil.

Timing was all important, Henri told her as he time and again checked the process. At last, Jacques, looking over Henri's shoulder, agreed with his protégé that the shade was perfect.

Quickly, Caren's head was over the sink and Henri removed the individual strips of foil, washing the bleach off before it could touch the rest of her hair.

Shampooed and rinsed, Caren gazed into the mirror seeing hardly any difference. "You cannot see the change so much when your hair is wet, *chérie*. But I assure you, it was well worth the inconvenience. When dry, your hair will seem to have lights of its own. And before the camera, it will soften your features, so."

"I believe you, Jacques." Her eyes met his in the mirror. "I'll always believe you." Remarkably, the Frenchman blushed.

When Henri had set her hair in huge rollers and tied a net around the whole works, he placed her under the dryer. Jacques solicitously brought her a plate with a delectable and appetizing array of fresh-cut vegetables and a yogurt dip accompanied by a cup of beef broth. "After your lunch the manicurist will attend you. If you need anything, anything at all, you are to ask Henri. No one else, do you understand, *chérie?* I have told Henri about my sin and your generosity. I assure you, he is now as devoted to you as I am."

Caren flushed, but accepted Jacques' statement and proffered lunch. She wouldn't think about those photos taken yesterday, and she wouldn't think about Moira Evans. That little bridge would be crossed when she came to it.

Forty-five minutes later, her lunch consumed and her nails freshly painted a subtle shade of mocha, Caren sat before Henri's mirror.

"What is troubling you, mademoiselle? Has not Jacques warned you about frowning? Don't you like what you see?"

Caren laughed. "It's not that, Henri. And yes, Jacques warned me about frowning. It's just that I don't think I've looked at myself in the mirror as much in my whole life as I have in the past two days."

"Ah!" the Frenchman soothed. "At least you have something very pretty to look at." He gently removed the rollers from Caren's hair and picked up his brush. Again and again, the soothing bristles stroked through her hair, taking away that tight-scalp feeling she always experienced when sitting under a dryer. Again and again, the brush ran through her hair, brushing it forward, brushing it back.

"Now, shake your head, mademoiselle. Like this, so your hair lifts away from your face. That's right."

Marveling, Caren watched as the light caught her hair. There were indefinable streaks so subtle they reminded her of how her hair had looked when she was a child and had spent the summer in the sun. And the haircut she had had the day before had added fullness and body; no matter which way she tossed her head, her hair fell in exquisite lines framing her face. "Is that me?" she asked incredulously.

"*Oui,* mademoiselle. It has always been you."

The warmth in Henri's voice brought color to her cheeks, but it was Jacques' wholehearted praise of her and his protégé's work that broke her into laughter. Happily, she followed Jacques back to the makeup room where he applied his tints and powders according to the notes he had made earlier. When he had finished, Caren had a hard time believing she was seeing herself. Not that the artistry of the Frenchmen had changed her—rather they had enhanced her, making her look vital, alive, and most of all, really pretty.

Jacques had been right. That particular shade of mulberry was perfection. She could see how if he had added a few grains of the darker color as Moira had wanted, she would have appeared gaunt. He had done a superb job, and she now felt more confident than ever. She still had that photographic session to get through with the handsome Marc Rayven in attendance, but she wouldn't let herself worry about that. Today, she had made great gains. Jacques and Henri were her friends, and she now knew the role Moira Evans had intended to play in her new career as the Nightstar girl. As she had told Jacques, now that she knew the rules, she had a better chance of winning the game.

As she walked down the hall to Bill Valenti's studio, Caren was aware that her knees were shaking. She had to admit to herself that she was not looking forward to the working session. In fact, she was dreading it. Again, doubts assailed her, punishing her. Why did she keep having these wide mood swings, these vague stirrings that had no name?

The thought of Marc Rayven sitting on his perch somewhere in the darkness as he watched the photograph session was curdling her innards. She remembered the fury the day before when he had misinterpreted Bill Valenti's reasons for baring Caren's shoulder. In spite of her embarrassment, she had to admit that his protective instincts had thrilled her.

What would he be thinking today as he watched her pose? Would he remember how she had felt in his arms? Would his flesh tingle the way hers did when he thought about the touch of her lips and the way she had responded to him? She shook her head; not likely. She had only to remember his parting shot when he told her he wondered if her lips were as good for loving as they were for lying.

Suddenly, it all became clear to her. If she had had any doubts she didn't have any now. It was Moira who had revealed the information about the Nightstar line and Caren's role as the Nightstar girl. Another thought occurred to Caren. Moira had known that news photographers would be present, snapping pictures. News photos were in black and white. How smug Moira must be feeling, assured that those photos would be published making her look like...like the jaded harlot that had appeared in the photos Bill Valenti took that day. She had had no way of knowing that Jacques, feeling guilty about his part in Moira's plot, had corrected the makeup before she had gone home. The girl who appeared on Marc's arm at the preview would be as pretty as Jacques could make her.

Marc! A horrible thought struck her. Here she had been, little fool that she was, hoping that Marc would remember the kiss they had shared the night before. What if he sat through her photo session comparing her to Moira? If he did, how would she, Caren, fare? Second best?

"I don't want to be second best!" she muttered to herself.

"I, for one, don't blame you," said a cool, masculine voice in her ear.

Caren swung about sharply and fell right into Marc Rayven's outstretched arms. Marc's eyes seemed to be mocking her, and yet they were alive with something akin to speculation. He was making fun of her and enjoying it. Damn you, Marc Rayven, she seethed inwardly. If she had any delusions about the previous evening and its meaning to the handsome cosmetic king, they were shattered. She was just a means to an end. He was using her to prove a point to the members of the board in order to get them to back the Nightstar campaign.

Caren felt her eyes narrow as she stared up at the man towering over her. "You know what they say, you can't make a silk purse out of a sow's ear. I guess it goes with second best, that kind of thing."

Marc's eyes were slits as he stared at her before striding off. He made no comment, but his jaw had tightened and Caren noticed that his powerful hands—relaxed only seconds ago—were now balled into tight, angry-looking fists. He was gone. Even his walk looked angry,

Caren thought as she rounded the corner that would take her into the photography studio. It was evident that he knew just what she was talking about. The truth hurts, doesn't it, Mr. Rayven? Sow's ear, my foot. Indignation welled up in her as she made her way over coiled electrical wires and skirted hard wooden chairs.

It was a large studio. There were none of the comforts of the other studios and salons in the Rayven building. This was a working area with as little clutter as possible. Every conceivable light and tripod made seemed to be on the round stagelike platform. Scenery was piled haphazardly against every wall as were folding chairs. A large, stainless-steel coffeepot with a red light glowed from one corner of the room. It was perched precariously on a lopsided wooden chair with two slats missing from the backrest. A faint aroma of some flowery scent hung in the air. Caren sniffed, unable to name the elusive scent. It wasn't the Nightstar collection, of that she was sure.

Voices from the end of the room next to the lavatory reached her ears. She peered out against the lights, but couldn't distinguish any forms. The saccharine-sweet sound of Moira's voice seemed to hang in the still air of the studio.

Jacques said something, his accent unmistakable. She waited, drawing in her breath, for Marc Rayven to say something. He must be there.

Quietly, she seated herself, straining to hear the words from the far end of the room. Drat, only the tones could be heard; the words were indistinguishable from where she was sitting. To Caren's untrained ear Jacques sounded defensive, Moira petulant, and Rayven downright angry, but controlled. Her back stiffened when she heard the word "infant" bounce off the walls and come to rest at her well-shod feet. They were moving now in her direction, speaking normally of everyday things—things she was evidently allowed to hear. As if I care, she murmured under her breath.

"It might be a good idea if Caren attended the meeting this afternoon. I suggest, Moira, that you cancel it and reschedule it for 5:50. Nothing is ever solved or settled after a three-martini lunch. The ad men will be there so we might as well make use of everyone's time. We'll get good ideas, fresh approaches, because each of us will be doing our best in the short time we have. In other words, Moira," Marc Rayven said coldly, "everyone wants to get home as quickly as possible after a long working day, and the only way to do that is to come through in the time allotted. Make it a full hour meeting. This way everyone can still catch the commuter.

Caren said nothing as she watched the little byplay between Moira and her boss. Her model's face was impassive as she seated herself next to Caren and crossed her legs, deliberately hiking the skirt she wore to well above her knee. With the slit on both sides of her skirt, Caren didn't know why she bothered. She was no prude, but halfway up the thigh was a bit much. Evidently, Marc Rayven thought so, too, as he stared pointedly at the silky expanse of leg. Moira fidgeted a moment and then demurely pulled down her skirt and uncrossed her legs. She folded her hands primly in her lap and smiled innocently at the assembled men. Caren felt a grin tug at the corners of her mouth. She erased it, but not before Marc's eyes twinkled down at her. His expression clearly said: there is a time and a place for everything.

The camera session was grueling and brutal. When it was over, Caren had a healthy respect for the gorgeous cover girls who made it all seem so easy. She was exhausted from all the twisting and turning, the perching, the languid poses that must look natural. Henri and Jacques were always at her elbow as one series of shots went into the next. The costume changes were made at breakneck speed, leaving her trembling and shaky as she emerged from behind the dressing screen.

Raggedy Ann, she thought as she flopped onto one of the hard wooden chairs when the photographer called it quits. Caren removed one spike heel and then the other. A sigh escaped her as she massaged her weary feet. A single tear gathered in the corner of her left eye and trickled down her cheek. Impatiently, knowing it was a sign of exhaustion, she brushed at it and then sniffed. Damn, she had to blow her nose. She sniffed again.

"Something tells me," said an aloof voice, "that you used to wipe your nose on your sleeve when you were a kid, right?" Caren nodded miserably. "Here," Marc Rayven said holding out a snowy square of linen.

Caren felt annoyed. Why did he have such an uncanny knack of showing up at the most inopportune times? She accepted the chalky handkerchief and blew her nose lustily. "Actually, Mr. Rayven, I used to wipe my nose on the hem of my shirttails," she said with an angry edge to her voice. "That was a long time ago, however. Now, I'm all grown up."

Marc Rayven grinned. "I can see that. That you're all grown up, I mean."

He was mocking her again. Well, let him. "I'll return your handkerchief after I launder it."

He was still grinning. "No hurry, but I'll look forward to seeing you under social conditions again."

She must be improving if he was making a halfhearted effort to see her again. No, that was wrong. She was the golden goose, a tarnished golden goose; and she was definitely not going to lay any eggs, golden or otherwise. Carefully, she tucked the square of linen into her tote bag and leaned over to put on her shoes. "It's harder than I thought. I simply was not prepared for this. I think you should know that I'm doing my best, and if that isn't good enough, I'll understand if you want to replace me."

Marc Rayven's eyes narrowed and his face took on a cool, chiseled look. "I wouldn't think of it. Didn't you ever hear that old adage about changing horses in midstream? Regardless of the outcome, we're in this together. If you want to back out because the going is too tough, that's something else."

Together. He had said they were in this together—together, as in Rayven and herself. If he had meant to include the beautiful Moira, he would have said, *all of us* are in this together.

Caren's face stilled. "No, I don't want to back out. I just want you to understand that I am doing my best. I'm not a quitter. My best, Mr. Rayven, is all you can expect from me."

"I think we understand each other perfectly. If we don't get a move on, both of us are going to be late for the meeting. Come along, Caren. By the way, how would you like to stop and have a drink after the meeting? Or are you too tired? I would suggest dinner, but I have a previous appointment."

"How about a rain check?" Caren said pertly. Now, where had she gotten the nerve to say that?

"I hope that doesn't mean I have to wait for a literal rain." The old mocking tone was back in his voice. Caren imagined her turndown was Marc's first rejection by anyone of her gender. Just remember: ugly duckling, sow's ear. How she hated those words.

"I want to stop in the powder room; I'll catch up," Caren said breathlessly, hurrying away from him. Why did this man affect her this way? Why was it suddenly so difficult to breathe?

Six

In the lush velvet-and-brocade powder room Caren tossed her tote onto a lime-green chair and then stretched out on a matching chaise. Lord, she was tired. Exhausted was too tame a word for the way she felt. The klieg lights had literally drained every ounce of her energy. She glanced at her watch and saw that she had exactly seventeen minutes to get to the meeting in Marc Rayven's office. Forty winks, forty cat winks. When she had been in school cramming for an exam, all she had had to do was repeat over and over "Seventeen minutes, seventeen minutes," till her eyes closed and then she would wake up right on the dot. It had always worked for her before, even when her alarm had blitzed out on her just over a month ago. It would work this time too; she was sure of it. Her eyes were so heavy, so very heavy. Just seventeen minutes. The thick black lashes fluttered wearily and then lay like gossamer webs on her cheeks.

Caren stirred once and forced her lids open. She still had seven minutes. How tired she was. Seven minutes more—an eternity at this moment. The feathery lashes closed again preventing her from seeing the shadowy form outlined in the doorway. Had she been awake, she would have seen the triumphant, malicious look on Moira Evans' face as she backed out of the doorway and closed the door quietly. No sound disturbed Caren's deep, even sleep.

The spiky hands of the sunburst clock read 6: 50 when angry voices could be heard coming down the hallway. Caren stirred fretfully and rolled over on her side. The chaise was too narrow and she was uncomfortable. Where were those angry voices coming from? Yawning heavily, she struggled to a sitting position trying to orient herself. Fearfully, she stared down at the gold circle on her wrist. It couldn't be! Her stricken eyes traveled to the sunburst clock and she winced as though in pain. It was! The meeting was over and she had missed it. Tears gathered in her eyes. Lord, she was tired. Vitamins— I should have started taking double doses of vitamins, she thought wearily as she grappled for her tote and a comb and brush.

The angry voices were getting nearer. Panic

gripped her and she ran into the lavatory part of the powder room. She knew she was behaving like a child, but was unable to stop herself. Quietly, she closed the stall door and then reopened it. She would not hide. Hadn't she just said she was all grown up? Grown-ups were responsible for their own actions. So she had fallen asleep. What could they do to her besides fire her?

Squaring her shoulders, ready to slay the proverbial dragon, Caren thrust open the swinging doors that led to the powder room and was just in time to hear Moira Evans say, "She must be asleep in here."

"On the contrary, Miss Evans, I just woke up. My apologies, Mr. Rayven. I hope you didn't wait too long to start the meeting. I have no excuse; I fell asleep and just woke a few minutes ago. Now, if you'll excuse me, I'll see you in the morning."

Was she mistaken or was that an amused look in Marc Rayven's eyes? Jacques, the photographer, and several distinguished-looking men with portfolios under their arms stared at her. No introductions were made, but then Caren had not given anyone time to do more than listen to her words. As she swept past Moira Evans she said, sotto voce, "If one had a mind to, one might wonder how you knew I was in here sleeping. One might also wonder why you didn't wake me.'' Without another glance in anyone's direction she was off, striding down the hall to the stairwell. There was no way she was going to stand waiting for an elevator and have to face all those people. Where in the world had she gotten the nerve to do what she had just done? For once in her life she had placed someone else on the defensive. Good, it was a step in the right direction.

The three-inch heels were in her hand as she tripped her way down eighteen floors. She was being silly and ridiculous, but she couldn't help herself. Besides, going down was easier than going up. Let them all wonder where she was and then mark it down to artistic temperament.

Carefully, Caren inched the ground-floor door open and peered outside. Satisfied that no one was about except the security guard, she still waited a full ten minutes before leaving. She whiled away the time considering Moira Evans' remark about her sleeping and the fact that she had opened the door to the powder room. Was it possible that she had seen Caren when she really was sound asleep and hadn't bothered to wake her, knowing that she would later embarrass her in front of the others? More likely than not. It was over and done with and she couldn't do a thing about it now.

Caren glanced at her watch again and then opened the door. She stepped out into the quiet lobby, her heels making the guard look up from his relaxed position behind the desk. She smiled and waved as she pushed at the revolving door.

The brisk evening air swept Caren down the street as she headed for her bus stop. The cobwebs in her brain were cleared by the refreshing winds of early fall. By the time she reached her tiny efficiency apartment she felt like an evening on the town. Her nap had definitely worked wonders, she grinned ruefully. But at what cost to herself? she wondered as she fit the key into the lock.

The phone shrilled demandingly as she sat down to eat her grilled cheese sandwich. She ignored it.

What's wrong with me? she asked herself querulously. Why am I having so much difficulty handling all of this? Is it because you're falling in love with Marc Rayven and he belongs to Moira Evans? a niggling voice asked.

Caren didn't like the direction in which her thoughts were traveling. There were no answers at the moment. Deftly, she wiped up the crumbs from the sandwich, carried her plate to the sink, and filled it with water. She finished the last of her tea and placed the cup carefully in the hot soapy water. She would clean up later.

The phone shrilled to life again as she stepped beneath the needle-sharp spray of the shower. It was ringing again when she wrapped herself in a faded fern-green terry robe. She padded into the small living room and reached for the receiver only to hear silence. So, they had given up. Persistence always won out in the end.

Caren knew it was ten o'clock because of the news program on television. The fifth commercial was in progress when there was a loud knock at her door. Caren froze with her hand in a bag of potato chips, her other hand holding a crisp red apple with two bites missing. A wave of panic coursed through her. Her buzzer hadn't sounded. Who could be knocking this late at night? Well, she wasn't going to answer it. A girl had to protect herself, living alone as she did. Police were forever warning single people not to open their doors to strangers. If nothing else, she was obedient, and not dressed for company. How would it look for the new Nightstar girl to open the door looking like a nightmare in real life? It wouldn't. Her decision made, she leaned back and took a third bite out of her shiny red apple. She chewed, unable to swallow the tart fruit.

"Caren, are you home? Caren, it's Marc Rayven. Open the door."

Oh no, it couldn't be Marc Rayven. But it was—she would know his voice if it was projected from the edges of eternity. She really was living under a black cloud, and it was descending rapidly. There was nothing to do but open the door and see what he wanted. Maybe he fired people in person instead of issuing pink slips.

The potato-chip bag scrunched under one arm, the apple in her left hand, she removed the chain and opened the door. She stepped back as Marc filled the doorway to overflowing. Her eyes were angry, her stance rigid as she stared into Marc Rayven's face. "Yes?" she said coolly, not bothering to invite him into the room.

"Yes what? Yes, I can come in? Just yes?"

"Come in, sit down." Her tone was less than gracious, but she couldn't help it. This was an intrusion on her privacy. He didn't own her, not quite. And this was definitely after business hours.

"Are you going to share?"

Caren frowned. "Share what?"

"Either or. Either the apple or the potato chips."

Was he mocking her again? She couldn't tell. He seemed for the moment just like any other guy that stopped by to see his girl. Only I'm not his girl, she thought unhappily. She flushed and held out the crackly bag of chips.

"Did you have any dinner?" she questioned.

Marc grinned. "Is it that obvious? I *didn't* have any dinner and I'm starved. I know this is an imposition, but do you have anything to eat? I'll do the dishes." The light banter seemed to relieve the tension between them.

Caren laughed in spite of herself. "I think I might be able to manage something. How about an omelet and some sausage?"

"Sounds great. Can I help?"

"If you want to eat, you help," she told him frankly. "You can get the dishes out."

Marc followed her into the tiny kitchen and she pointed to the cupboard where she kept the plates. As she was frying the sausage and whipping the eggs, Marc helped himself to a glass of milk and pushed the toast down into the toaster. "Ummm," he savored, "smells like breakfast."

"Or it will if you plug in the coffeepot," she told him.

Following her orders, Marc plugged in the pot and sat down at the table. She could feel his eyes watching her as she prepared his meal. Beneath his scrutiny, she burned her fingers twice, spilled grease on the stove, and dropped the butter knife as she was spreading jam on the toast.

"Are you always so graceful, Miss Ainsley?" he mocked.

"Always," she assured him, returning his sarcasm. "Just remember, he who finds complaint finds work. Would you like to prepare your own dinner?"

"Nope. I'd rather just sit here and watch you."

That last remark brought color to Caren's cheeks. Suddenly, she was aware of her freshly scrubbed face—completely devoid of Jacques' artistry—and her nudity beneath the faded green robe. Even her bare feet sticking out from under the long wrapper caused her embarrassment. She should have run and changed almost the minute he arrived, but she hadn't and it was too late to do it now without feeling foolish.

When Caren dished out the omelet for Marc,

he seemed surprised. "Where's yours? You're not going to make me eat alone, are you?"

"Well, you see, Mr. Rayven, the company I work for has put me on this strict diet, and since I've already cheated by eating a sandwich earlier, I think I'll just have coffee while you eat."

"A diet!" he snorted. "That's ridiculous! You're just perfect the way you are. If I'd wanted one of those emaciated fashion models, I would have gotten one. As your employer, I order you, right this minute, to forget about the diet." With great ceremony, he pulled her plate over and pushed half his omelet and a slice of sausage onto it. "And an omelet is never complete without toast. Here, it's the one with extra jelly."

Giggling, Caren happily bit into the toast, dribbling a spot of jelly on her chin. Marc laughed and wiped it off for her.

The rest of the meal was spent in easy camaraderie as they discussed the plans for the Nightstar line, and Caren was very flattered that Marc was truly sincere in hearing her opinions.

After they had drained their coffee cups twice, Marc stood up and began to clear the table.

"What are you doing?"

"I told you I would do the dishes and I meant it."

It was on the tip of her tongue to protest, saying something trite like that was woman's work when she remembered the articles she had read in magazines. There was no such thing as woman's work or man's work either. If you were capable of doing it, then you should do it. "All right then, since you did promise—" she turned on her heel and walked into the living room.

"Would you mind turning the TV set on to the Public Broadcasting System—Channel Thirteen. The Boston Pops Symphony Orchestra is having a gala tonight and John Williams is conducting."

Doing as he requested, Caren sat on the floor in front of the TV. Really fine reception wasn't usual on Channel Thirteen, but she would fine-tune it and do her best. Funny, she thought to herself, when it came to Marc Rayven, she was always giving her best.

The clatter of pots and pans sounded in the kitchen and Caren laughed when Marc walked out to the table to retrieve the coffee cups, wearing the little apron she always kept tied to the refrigerator handle.

"What's so funny?" he demanded.

"You are." She continued laughing. "You...you look so silly—"

"Oh, I do, do I?" A threat was in his voice and in his blue eyes.

"Yes—"

"I'll show you how silly I am." There was a definite threat in his tone now, a teasing menace. His fingers untied the little apron with great deliberateness. Cool blue eyes watched her, measured her, yet there was a hidden bank of fires within them, and Caren was mesmerized by the budding desire she saw in them.

Slowly, step by step, he came toward her, his eyes holding her, hypnotizing her, making it impossible for her to move. Dimly, she was aware of her vulnerability, of her nudity beneath the heavy terry-cloth robe.

He was near her now, near enough to reach out and touch her. She felt herself shrink away from him, yet there was something, some inner part of her that wanted to make her throw herself into his arms and plead for mercy—later, much later.

From her position on the floor she looked up at him, realizing how he towered over her, making her feel small and defenseless. By the dim lights in the room she saw his eyes were alight with desire, the desire he had shown her in the tiny vestibule the night before. His sensually curving lips were grim with a raw hunger, and the stubborn set of his jaw told her that she was facing a power that she was helpless to control.

Even as she shrank away from him, his gaze held her. Slowly, intractably, he extended his hand, compelling her to take it, to allow herself to be lifted to her feet, to fall into his arms. With a will that was not her own, she reached out tentative fingers, allowing him to grasp them in his, allowing him his wish.

His dark hair fell forward over his brow, lending him a boyish look. Heavy dark brows were drawn together over the bridge of his straight, classic nose. He was a handsome devil and devilish in his desires. His white business shirt was open at the neck, revealing the corded strength of him. As she stood before him, a struggle was evident in his eyes and then, with a deep, broken sound, he seized her and buried his face against her throat.

If Marc Rayven was the devil, then she, Caren, was his advocate. She tumbled into his arms, willingly, reveling in the passion behind his caress. Her body throbbed to the sound of her name upon his lips.

He was an enigma of a man. At once he was tender and at the same time demanding. She realized, with a joyful helplessness, that she was powerless to escape his strength. His will became her own as he evoked her responses with a fiery awakening. His kisses and caresses were inspired; he knew instinctively her little pleasure points where he pressed his lips, his breath hot, scorching her skin, giving her a pleasure she had never known existed for her.

His arms swept her up, his mouth still possessing hers, and he carried her to the wide, chocolate-brown couch. The implications of this movement made her heart pound, made her body quiver with expectation. She should fight, she should protest, but despite knowing what she *should* do, her arms twined around his neck, betraying her. Her emotions were traitorous, succumbing to the wicked power he held over her. In a vague recess of her mind she knew she would be sorry in the morning, but those thoughts were swept away by a wild, pounding need—a need, a thirst, that could only be quenched in the arms of Marc Rayven.

The edges of her robe fell apart, exposing an expanse of creamy skin to his lips, his hands. She throbbed at his every touch as his fingers grazed the hollows of her throat and the gentle curves of her breasts. He was taking her on a journey into the unknown, but as long as he held her, touched her, she was unafraid. She sought the heights his nearness promised, demanded the fulfillment she knew could be hers.

A ringing sounded in her head, sharp and insistent. Again, it sounded, jarring her, making her want to escape it, to hide forever in the arms of her love.

With a strange kind of relieved dismay, Caren realized at the same time as Marc that the ringing was not in their heads, but that it was the phone. With a mournful sigh, Marc lifted himself from the couch and went to the far side of the room to answer it.

"Yes?" he answered angrily, no doubt forgetting that this was Caren's apartment and Caren's phone and that the call could very well be for her.

"Not now, Moira—"

Moira Evans. Of course, Caren thought, pulling the edges of her robe together, suddenly feeling very exposed and vulnerable and, yes, wicked.

"I didn't think I had to report to you where I would be this evening, Moira, and I *don't* intend to do so in the future. You'd better be calling to tell me about a crisis at the firm; otherwise, I don't want to hear it.'' He paused, listening for a moment. His simple response was a puzzled, ''Oh.'' He then turned to Caren. ''Moira. She wants to talk to you.'' He held out the receiver and awkwardly, Caren crossed the room, tightening the belt on her robe and pulling the collar up around her neck. Her eyes refused to meet Marc's, refused to lift themselves to look into the eyes of the man she was certain she had fallen in love with, the man who just a moment ago had been holding her in his arms and awakening passions in her she had never dreamed she could experience.

Putting the receiver to her ear, she still kept her eyes glued to the floor. ''Yes...yes,'' she managed with more assurance.

''Is that you, Miss Ainsley?'' Moira's nasty voice hissed in her ear.

''Sp-speaking.''

Marc had moved away from her. She watched as, never turning for a backward glance, he picked up his jacket and coat from the easy chair and moved toward the door. He held himself stiffly, determinedly, opening the door and closing it behind him. No explanation, nothing. He had just left—gone. And somehow, not knowing how, Caren had the feeling that he was walking out of her life forever.

"Don't talk, just listen," the voice on the phone instructed. "I know what little game you're playing, and believe me when I tell you it won't work. Marc Rayven has no place in his life for a nondescript little typist. He's out of your league. You mean nothing more to him than the last Rayven Cosmetics model he sported around town. I'm giving you fair warning. Stay away from Marc, he belongs to *me*. He always has. Do you understand?"

Crestfallen, feeling abandoned and alone, Caren's eyes tried to bore through the thick wood of the door. If only she could see him, know what he was thinking, she would have the courage to tell Moira Evans where to get off. Instead, feeling defeated, desolate, and rejected, she placed the telephone receiver back on its cradle.

Visions of herself and Marc stretched out on the couch, his hands worshiping her body, his lips promising love, blurred before Caren's eyes. Yes, she definitely understood what Moira was saying. Her face flushed a bright scarlet as she thought about what she had almost allowed to happen between herself and Marc. No, that was wrong. He wasn't Marc, he was Mr. Rayven, her employer—nothing more. Regardless of what her heart wanted to believe, regardless of the white heat her body had experienced, Moira was right; Marc Rayven *was* out of Caren's league.

Her eyes were fixed on the door, still seeing Marc's back turned to her. A silent tear slid down her cheek and touched the corner of her mouth, seeming to cool the warmth where Marc had touched it with his own.

Seven

More determined than ever, Caren literally put her nose to the grindstone and worked long, exhausting hours in the days and weeks that followed Marc Rayven's abrupt departure. By the minicalendar on her night table she figured that it was seventeen days since she had last seen Marc. Seventeen long, miserable days. She admitted now to herself in the privacy of her bedroom late at night that she loved Marc—for all the good it was going to do her. If she had mattered to him, he never would have left her that night seventeen days ago. One call from Moira and he was off and running like one of those long-distance runners who were always showing up on the evening news programs.

Three weeks to the day of her last meeting with Marc Rayven, Caren woke with a strange feeling. Today was her last day with the commercials. Today was the day the first series of commercials was going to be shown to the Rayven executives and the ad agency. Moira had seemed edgy and out of sorts the night before when she'd reminded Caren to be in the screening room promptly at ten A.M. As if wild horses or the devil himself could keep her away, even if it was her day off—the promised day off that she had looked forward to for the past month. A day to do whatever she pleased. Some luck, she mused as she applied a light layer of makeup in the way Jacques had taught her. Six one-minute commercials. Another hour to discuss the pros and cons and she would be free to do as she pleased. At the last minute she plucked a tiny vial from her purse and dabbed the new Nightstar perfume behind her ears and at the base of her throat. The minuscule cylinder without benefit of a label had been a gift from Marc, sent by him to the studio.

The hastily written note had said, "I believe this small offering is worthy of you." He could have turned that statement around and said she might be worthy of the precious perfume; but he hadn't, and the message had lifted her spirits a little. Still, on the other hand, she grimaced to herself, he could merely have been protecting his investment.

Why, oh why, did she always have to allow such negative thoughts to creep into her mind? Why couldn't she just accept her success and live on a day-to-day basis like all of the other career girls whom she had met in the last weeks? Because success, money, prestige, meant nothing unless you had someone close to you to share the feelings with. And always those hateful words "sow's ear" would ring in her ears reminding her of who and what she was.

One last look in the bathroom mirror that hung on the back of the door and she would be ready to leave. Her weight was stable now, thanks to the high-protein diet the nutritionist had put her on. Personally, she hadn't liked the thin, elegant look she was presenting to the world. And she hadn't felt all that well. The vitamins she was now taking were helping somewhat, but she still felt tired all the time. Visions of food, rich and sweet, tantalized her dreams at night, prompting her to make trips to the refrigerator for celery stalks or carrot sticks. She was a perfect size nine now, and she planned to remain that size.

Caren stuck her tongue out at her reflection and then turned off the bathroom light. Just how well was that perfect size nine going to wear over the next grueling two-month tour of the United States?

All the way to the Rayven building she argued with herself. They had to give her a few days off before the tour started. They just had to. In her heart she knew Moira was pushing her, prodding her, hoping against hope that she would fizzle out and the promotion would go down the drain at the eleventh hour. Well, she had sworn to do her best and that was exactly what she was going to do. Moira could take a flying leap—and where she landed, Caren didn't care.

Marc, Marc, Marc, her mind sang quietly as she rode the elevator to the screening room. Surely he would be there for the preview of the commercials. Could she handle it? Of course. Now that she was the Nightstar girl she could handle anything—almost anything, she corrected herself.

The screening room looked like a miniature theater, and it was full to capacity when she arrived. A sellout performance, she thought wryly as she found a seat in the back row, hoping to go unnoticed. She wanted to sit alone in the darkness so she could look at herself objectively on the giant-size screen. It was not to be.

How could she have forgotten how tall he was

or how he made her feel? Her heart thumped maddeningly as Marc Rayven strode down the short aisle to where she was sitting. He stared down at her for a full moment before reaching down for her hand to draw her to her feet. "Front row, center, Caren." She nodded as she followed him down the aisle, not trusting her voice. If it was as shaky as her knees, he would know in a minute what his presence was doing to her.

A veil dropped over her eyes as she took her place next to Marc and Moira. Moira must never know how she felt about Marc. She risked a quick sideways glance at her and was shocked at the expression on her chiseled features. Why was she looking so satisfied, so...so happy? And Jacques, why was he looking so grim and determined? Marc was the only one who appeared to be his natural, cool self. Butterflies fluttered around in her stomach as she prepared herself for the moment the lights went down in the screening room. She forced herself to lean back in the deep scarlet chair and relax. If she was lucky, the commercials would be terrible; Marc would say, "Sorry, it's been a mistake," and then they would all tell her to go home.

By the time the lights came on, Caren was

stunned. The commercials were not like she had expected. That captivating, romantic creature on the screen couldn't have been Caren Ainsley! There had been closeups, certainly, and she hadn't had to say a word. She had moved through the scenes as though in a dream; the narrator's deep, articulate voice had done the selling of Nightstar. But she, herself, Caren, had epitomized the essence of the precious perfume.

Looking at it objectively now, she could appreciate the loveliness of the graceful, flowing gowns. Even the old Victorian mansion in one of the commercials had appeared to be a reality instead of a mock-up on the studio's stage. John Williams had composed the music and conducted the orchestra for the background. In another of the commercials, swirls of fog had seemed to lift off the black waters of a New England seaport and waft around her feet. The London Fog raincoat's collar had been pulled high around her neck, and her hair, Henri's artwork, had been pulled back—only tender little tendrils allowed to escape around her face and neck.

The Nightstar theme was deeply romantic. It was the portrayal of every woman's daydreams. In the film clips Caren was always alone—alone with her Nightstar perfume. But the impression was always given that romance and that spe- cial someone were just around the corner, and with Nightstar—and Nightstar alone—romance wouldfind a woman ready and waiting.

Caren's thoughts came back to the present. All around her, voices were babbling; there was much backslapping and high-geared camaraderie being shared. Marc was kissing her resoundingly and telling her that he knew, he just knew, that she was exactly what Nightstar needed.

"Congratulations," Moira said evenly, breaking the spell between Caren and Marc as she held out her hand to Caren. Caren stood still, refusing to accept the handshake. Marc stared first at Caren and then at Moira, seeming to notice for the first time the look of abject fury in his assistant's eyes. At first, Caren thought he was going to say something, and then one of the advertising executives drew him away out of earshot of the stunning Moira.

"Thank you," Caren said quietly, still not bothering to extend her hand. Short of looking foolish, Moira had no other choice but to withdraw her hand and walk away. Caren watched her weave her way toward Jacques Duval. She waited, watching the expression on Jacques' face change as he waited for Moira to walk up to him. Either the Frenchman was talking through clenched teeth or he was listening to Moira; Caren couldn't tell. Whatever was going on, it appeared to Caren that Jacques was not giving an inch in Moira's direction.

"I'm sorry, that was business," Marc said drawing Caren off to the side. "Let me say that the commercials were better than any of us even hoped for. What did you think of them?"

Men! He hadn't seen her for weeks, and all he could think of was the commercials. What about the night in my apartment? her mind wanted to shriek. Was all of that a dream? Didn't it mean anything to you? She couldn't say any of those things. Now, she had to play the game. Well, it took two to play any kind of game. She chose her words carefully. "It's just my personal opinion, of course, but I think the commercials prove that you can indeed make a silk purse out of a sow's ear." She was shocked at how calm and matter-of-fact her voice was.

Marc Rayven's eyes narrowed to slits as he stared down at Caren. At best, his voice was chilly. "I don't know exactly what that's supposed to mean, probably one of those womanly remarks that men are not supposed to understand. Now, if you would be so gracious as to give the ad boys a few moments of your time, they want to go over your itinerary for the tour. You leave in three days. Moira has offered to be your traveling companion. I'll meet up with you along the way from time to time to keep an eye on things. Come along," he said taking hold of her arm. Deftly, Caren shook off his hand and moved back a step.

"Unfortunately, Mr. Rayven, your suggestion, or your order, is entirely unacceptable. I cannot be ready to leave for at least a week. I need time to rest. Your assistant, or whatever she is to you, will *not* be my companion. I am not being uncooperative. If you feel the need to assign me a companion or someone to watch over the image you created, you will have to find someone else. That, Mr. Rayven, is my bottom line—a week. I promised you my best, and I cannot give my best without some time off to get myself back together."

The chilly voice was now frost-tipped as were Marc Rayven's eyes. "You have a contract, and it calls for you to be in Dallas, Texas, at the Neiman Marcus store in three days' time."

"Mr. Rayven, I think you just created a problem for yourself. Please extend my apologies to

Mr. Neimen and Mr. Marcus and tell them I cannot possibly be there. My bottom line, Mr. Rayven. And don't put this down to artistic temperament. Put it down to overwork, twenty-four-hour hostility, hunger, and sleepless nights."

"These plans can't be changed. If you don't show up or we're forced to change the schedule, the whole damned tour is fouled up. You must honor your contract."

"Mr. Rayven," Caren said hotly, "you may own and operate this company and you may hold your contract over my head all you want, but it won't change things. A week—and without your assistant. My best was all I ever promised you." Now, make whatever you want out of that, Caren thought miserably.

"We'll discuss this later. The agency people are waiting for you," Marc said tightly. "I don't have time to play with your emotional temperament at the moment. My bottom line is you have a contract and you damned well better plan on honoring it. Because if you don't, you'll never work in this city again, and by that I mean you won't even be able to get a job as a salesgirl in the dime store. That's my bottom line." Without another word he strode from the room, a murderous look on his face.

People were staring at her, wondering what she was going to do. Evidently, all eyes had been on the two of them during the heated discussion. Smile, she had to smile and pretend everything was all right. Well, damn it, it wasn't all right. How dare he threaten her! Who did he think he was? Just the creator of the silk purse. And now he thought he owned her. Did he care if she fell on her face from exhaustion? Did he care if Moira was out to get her scalp? All he was interested in was his perfume. Well, she was going to have to make the best of it for the moment or else create a scene that she might come to regret later.

I must have a dual personality, she thought as she talked with the advertising people about her schedule. She smiled, said the right things, allowing them to think she would be in Texas in three days. What kind of gutless wonder am I to do this? she asked herself over and over as she accepted one compliment after another. At the end of the second hour she still hadn't made her intentions known to the agency. Moira was always on the fringes of the group, listening to the conversations and saying little herself.

Caren had six invitations for lunch, all of which she turned down. She was going to stop by the deli and pick up a loaf of sourdough bread, a stick of sweet butter, and a jar of black-raspberry jam, go home and eat the whole thing. After which she would wash it all down with two cans of soda. So there, Marc Rayven.

How could he stand there and talk to her the way he had after that evening they had spent together? Because it didn't mean anything to him, that's how, she answered herself. So much for all of her bravado back in the screening room, she thought as she raced through the lobby on her way home. She knew she was going to do as ordered. Why hadn't she just accepted it and let it go? Oh no, she had to go and give her own ultimatum and make a fool of herself.

And all because her pride was hurt; all because she had fallen in love with Marc Rayven. Fallen in love with a man who didn't or wouldn't return her feelings. The only thing the cosmetics king was interested in was Caren Ainsley, the commodity, who would sell his cosmetics.

All the way home she chastised herself. She was still tearing herself apart when she entered the deli for her treat. Her packages under her arm, her mouth drooling, she walked the rest of the way home, mentally savoring each bite of the still-warm bread under her arm.

The kitchen clock read 2:15 when Caren ate the last slice of the rich sourdough bread. The jam jar contained a half teaspoon of jam. The butter was a thing of the past. One soda can was resting in the trash and the other had barely a sip left.

"I feel like a balloon," Caren muttered to the empty kitchen, "and I feel guilty. It's just that I've been eating that rabbit food for so long I had to get something starchy and sweet or go out of my mind." There was a look of disgust on her face—disgust with herself when she was forced to open the button on her skirt. Gutless wonder that she was, she had given in to her basic urges, the need for food, real food. Basic urges. How wonderful they were when two people agreed. Gut-level basics. Now, she was feeling sorry for herself.

Her lower lip trembled as she remembered the evening she had cooked for Marc and those intimate moments later. Tears gathered in her eyes and slowly trickled down her cheeks. Was it her fault that she was a virginal sow's ear? Was it really? A giggle rose in her throat. That wasn't quite true anymore. Now, she was a virginal silk purse, heavier by at least five pounds since her binge in the kitchen. So I'll just have celery and lettuce with lemon juice for dinner, and I'll exercise for two hours, she pacified herself. Now she would take a nice leisurely bath and then a nap. She would need all of her strength to chew on the celery and for the exercises she would do later.

Ten o'clock the next morning found Caren sleeping dreamlessly in her lonely bed. The beginning of the night had been a torment. Thoughts of Marc Rayven plagued her. Arguments with herself about what she had said and what she should have said rolled around in her weary brain. She had fallen asleep at last, holding the conviction that she should have told Marc Rayven exactly where he could get off, that she would not make her public-appearance debut in Texas or anywhere else, for that matter. She was tired, exhausted, and needed some time to get her act together. Aside from the fact that she wasn't relishing the thought of days at hard labor in front of the camera and making personal appearances, for which she had no background, it was the principle of the thing.

Just who did Mr. Rayven think he was to threaten her that way? Telling her she wouldn't be able to get a job in the local five-and-dime! As if New York was the last city on earth. As if she couldn't move, find a life somewhere else.

It was impossible. Caren Ainsley wasn't the kind of girl to do anything by half measures. Her contract with Rayven Cosmetics was binding. She had signed it. She would live up to it, whatever the cost to herself—and her pride.

When the intercom buzzed, Caren groaned, rolling over between the sheets, clinging desperately to sleep. Wonderful, escapist, peaceful sleep. Again, the intercom buzzed. Again. Again.

Whoever it was, was certainly insistent. Climbing out from under her nice warm covers, she padded into the living room and pressed the button on the intercom. "Yes?" she questioned sleepily.

"Caren? That you? Don't tell me you were still sleeping on a beautiful day like this?" his deep, masculine voice inquired. "Push the buzzer, I'm coming up!"

What was Marc Rayven doing here at this

time of day? He should be hard at work in his office, especially after yesterday's viewing of the commercials they had shot.

"Caren? Do you hear me? Push the buzzer, I'm coming up! I'll give you one more minute and then I'm going to the superintendent." His tone was harsh, insistent, grating on her nerves. The one thing she did not need this morning was another confrontation with the Lipstick King.

"Go away," she managed weakly. "I'm not ready to see anyone."

"You open this door this minute. You hear?"

"Yes, I hear. And must I remind you that to-day is my day off and I don't have to take orders from you."

"I just want to be certain you're all right. You sound so out of it," he protested, softening his tone a little.

"I assure you I am fine. I sound out of it because you got me out of bed. I was sleeping. And no, I do not feel guilty for spending the morning in bed. I need my beauty rest, remember? Now, go away."

"Open this door! Or else I'll get the key from the super. I'll tell him that I'm your big brother and that I'm worried about you. Or I could tell him I'm your husband and you're my runaway bride; or I could say—''

Disgusted, Caren pressed the little black button, cutting off his words, electrically opening the door downstairs in the tiny vestibule.

Pushing her hair back from her face, Caren's first impulse was to dash back into the bedroom and brush her teeth, comb her hair, and get dressed. Then she thought better of it. Anyone who came unannounced first thing in the morning deserved what he got. Instead, she padded into the kitchen and began preparing a pot of coffee. She had no sooner snapped on the plastic lid and replaced the coffee can in the refrigerator, than the doorbell of her apartment sounded.

''Who is it?'' she called through the door.

''You know very well who it is. Now let me in!''

She snapped the locks and turned the knob and there, before her, was Marc Rayven burdened down with dozens of flowers. ''Help me out, will you? I've carried these things for twelve blocks and my arms are about to fall off.''

Caren relieved him of three bouquets and watched, openmouthed, as he dumped the rest uneceremoniously onto the kitchen table. "I wanted to surprise you." He grinned sheepishly.

"You did, you did." She smiled, burying her nose in the myriad chrysanthemums and daisies intermingled with the sweetest of pale pink roses. She noticed that this was the first time she had seen Marc dressed in anything besides carefully tailored suits and white shirts and ties. This morning he sported a denim jacket lined with sheepskin and faded blue jeans over tall Frye boots.

"I really did get you out of bed, didn't I?"

"I've already told you that. Was the purpose of this visit simply to deliver these flowers? What's happened? Is FTD on strike or something?" she asked sarcastically. If he thought he could buy her cooperation with flowers he was mistaken.

"I wanted to see your face when I gave them to you."

"You've seen it, Mr. Rayven. What else?"

"That coffee I smell. I'm starving. Skipped breakfast this morning."

"I don't believe I invited you, Mr. Rayven."

"But you will, won't you?" He laughed, as arrogant and confident as ever.

"First tell me why all the flowers."

"Because you're terrific. The viewing was a total success yesterday but I never had the chance to congratulate you. Not properly, anyway. Now, where're the cups?"

"Top shelf, right side of the sink. But why so many? Flowers, I mean?"

"Because, Miss Ainsley, you are more, much more than I ever hoped for in my Nightstar girl. You are wonderful and maybe flowers can convey what words can't. Sugar, where's the sugar?"

"On the table, under the roses. And you came all the way over here just to tell me that? And to bring flowers? I don't have nearly enough vases to put them in. They'll die!"

"Do you take milk? Where's your frying pan. I'm going to make some eggs." He removed his heavy denim jacket and tossed it over a chair. "How do you like them?"

"They're beautiful. I've never had so many flowers given to me at one time!" Caren exclaimed, removing a green glass vase from the top of the refrigerator.

"Not the flowers, the eggs. How do you like your eggs?"

"Sunnyside." She ran water from the tap into the vase. "I'm not going to have enough vases.

You're incredible! How did you know I loved daisies?''

"Bacon?''

"Don't you think about anything but food? It's in the meat tray, bottom left. And while you're at it, I'll have two pieces of toast. If you're going to undo my diet, might as well go all the way.''

"Go get dressed,'' Marc ordered abruptly. "And dress warmly, it's getting cold just the way the middle of October should. But not too fancy. I just feel like bumming today.''

She found her steps taking her to the bedroom to obey his orders, her mind already sorting through her wardrobe for something plain and warm. Suddenly, she stopped dead in her tracks. "Hey, you can't come in here and help yourself to breakfast and then order me to get dressed and even tell me what to wear! Who do you think you are anyway?''

"I'm the guy who's frying your bacon. I'm also the guy who lets you bring home the bacon, if you get my meaning. Now get dressed!''

"No!'' She stamped her foot, really angry now. "I will not! This is my home and I'll get dressed—''

The words stuck in her throat. Marc had

tossed down the spatula and was stalking toward her. There was a threat in his eyes and a determination about his mouth. "Are you going to get in there and get dressed or do I have to do it for you?" Closer he came, his arms reaching for her. Caren had no doubt but that he would do it, adding humiliation to her anger.

With a shriek that should have brought the house down, she raced into her bedroom, slamming the door shut. Before she realized, she was laughing, boisterously, uproariously.

"And don't forget to wash behind your ears," he yelled through the door. "I'm going to check!"

When Caren stepped shyly out from the bedroom, she was wearing designer jeans that had been part of her wardrobe for a camera sitting and a thick soft yellow mohair pullover. Her hair, streaked by Henri, was tied casually at the back of her head, soft wispy tendrils escaping onto her cheeks and brow. She hadn't applied any makeup except a touch of mascara and a smear of lip gloss. Today was her day off and she wanted to be Caren Ainsley, not the Nightstar girl.

In the kitchen, her breakfast was waiting for her. Also, every available pitcher and deep pot were in use as vases for the meadow of flowers he had brought with him. The air was filled with the unlikely combination of coffee, bacon, and roses.

"Good, you're dressed warm. It's going to be cold where we're going." His voice was approving. "And by the way, Miss Ainsley, did anyone ever tell you that you're perfectly lovely in the morning?"

Caren flushed, the hand holding her coffee cup trembling slightly. Why could this man do this to her? His very presence in the room could set her nerves tingling, turning her into a bumbling idiot. Then the full meaning of his words settled on her consciousness. "Where we're going?"

"You do have three days off, don't you? Hurry up and finish your breakfast. I'll clean up the dishes while you pack."

"Pack?"

"Yes pack, Miss Ainsley. You'll be needing sturdy shoes, we're going to walk through the woods—and a jacket, a thick warm one. And of course, nightgowns and don't forget your toothbrush." He bit into his toast, the sound crunching in the quiet.

"I—I don't know.... Didn't you tell me the

tour began in Texas? That's three days from now. I—I wasn't planning on…No! The answer is definitely no! My contract states—"

"Eat!" he ordered. "You are not packing for business, Caren. I'm taking you to my place in the Pocono Mountains. It's only about two hours from Manhattan. Pennsylvania. You *have* heard of Pennsylvania, haven't you?"

"Yes, of course. But I don't understand."

"Did you or did you not tell me yesterday how exhausted you are? Didn't you tell me you wanted time to get yourself together? Some time for yourself? Well, I've arranged it—and the woods are beautiful at this time of year. You're going to love it. Now eat!"

Chewing on her bacon, Caren watched him as he forked his egg. She wasn't certain she liked the idea of being sent to the mountains. Wasn't she allowed to make any decisions for herself anymore? "I don't want to go. I was planning on staying right here. Do some reading—"

"You can do all that in the mountains. Plus, you can enjoy a change of scene. You can walk through the woods. It's perfect." He challenged her with his eyes, daring her to protest again.

"I—I don't want to go. I won't like being all alone in a strange place—"

"Caren," he said, touching her hand with his fingertips. "You won't be alone. I'll be there with you. Please, I'm asking you. Won't you come away with me? I can promise you'll love it. Or is it that you don't want to be with me after—after the last time we were together?" He watched her; she could feel his gaze penetrate her very being, staining her cheeks pink as the roses he had brought her.

"Please, Caren. It will be good for both of us." How could she deny him anything, this man who could set her pulse racing just by talking to her? The pleading in his tone was a total departure from the way he usually barked commands. Deciding the time had come for her to ignore everything other than what she really wanted, Caren looked up at him. What she wanted, more than anything else on this earth, was to go away with Marc Rayven.

While Caren was in the bedroom packing, Marc, true to his word, was in the kitchen doing the dishes. She couldn't help thinking of what a paradox this man was. On the one hand he was a cosmetics mogul, barking orders, making decisions, running a multimillion-dollar business. On the other, he wasn't afraid to do what some men would call "women's work." There he was this very minute, humming along to the radio and sudsing away bacon grease.

Into the suitcase Caren folded several sweaters and another pair of jeans. A robe and slippers and her favorite talcum powder followed. On impulse, just in case, she added a long black silk skirt, a vibrant blue silk blouse, a gold chain belt, panty hose, and velvet strap evening slippers. She hoped she wouldn't have to wear them, but it was good to know she would have them. Marc's moods were sometimes so mercurial, there was no telling if he would decide to have dinner out at some fancy restaurant. She remembered the casual ease he had displayed when he had taken her to lunch at the Russian Tea Room, even convincing them to stay open past the lunch hour. For good measure, she added a tiny black beaded evening purse. The small makeup kit that Jacques had put together for her contained all the essentials yet was compact and easy to carry. Adding brush, comb, and toothbrush, she snapped the lid on the suitcase.

"Ready? Good girl. That was quick; some women would take half the day deciding on this or that. You're a marvel, Caren." Marc beamed. "Kitchen's all done. Anything else?"

Caren peeked into the kitchen. "You're the

marvel, Marc. You really are. You did that in record time. What's your secret?''

"Organization. That's all there is to it.''

"No sense in puffing your chest out, Mr. Rayven. You haven't accomplished the impossible, you know. We women do the same little chore day in and day out." There, that should deflate him somewhat. She couldn't allow him to think that cleaning a few dishes was the eighth wonder of the world. Her eye fell on a pot lid still on top of the stove. Before he could stop her, she picked it up and opened the oven door. New York apartments were always short on cabinet space and the oven was as good a place as any to store pots and pans.

The oven door swung open and out clattered a dirty frying pan. Startled, she peered inside. There were the coffeepot, the dishes—

"You didn't do the dishes!" she accused. "You just stuffed everything in the oven!"

"Come on, let's get going." He grabbed her by the elbow and steered her toward the door. "We'll worry about the dishes when we get back."

A last backward glance at the kitchen made Caren cringe. She knew that the "we" Marc spoke of was going to be "she."

Outside the apartment building, Marc's shiny red sports car was parked at the curb—illegally. A stiff white card was stuck under his windshield wiper. "Look Marc, they've given you a ticket."

"It's not the first and it won't be the last." He shrugged, pushing it into the pocket of his slim, skin-fitting jeans.

"Just a second. I thought you said you walked twelve blocks carrying those flowers. How come your car is parked so conveniently outside my apartment?" She lifted a suspicious eyebrow, liking the way he was squirming.

"How else was I going to gain your sympathy so you'd let me have breakfast with you?" He smiled, his dark hair tumbling over his brow giving him a "Peck's Bad Boy" look.

"You might have tried asking," she said sternly, handing him her suitcase so he could stow it behind the front seats along with his own.

"Next time, I promise. Hop in, it's getting late and I want to show you my woods around the cabin."

The ride was soothing, delectable, but whenever she glanced over to see Marc driving beside her, little shivers would run up her spine. He was so masterful, so confident, handling the car like a pro. Even when the traffic was thick, crossing over the George Washington Bridge, she was completely at ease with Marc at the wheel.

Once outside the metropolitan area traffic was lighter and they spun down the road, the sun streaming through the windshield, warming the interior of the car. Or was it just being so close to Marc that made her feel this way—warm and drugged with contentment?

The mountains loomed before them, the sun touching the gold and red leaves and bringing them to glory. The radio played and they sang along with old familiar tunes, happy to be in one another's company.

Lunch was eaten at a wayside hot-dog stand and they both vowed they were the best hot dogs they'd ever eaten.

It was shortly after two in the afternoon when Marc pulled onto a side road and the sports car hugged the side of the mountain as they made the climb. Caren's ears popped halfway up and still the car climbed, high into the clouds.

When at last Marc pulled into the long, winding driveway, Caren found herself looking ahead, into the distance, for her first glimpse of the house. Marc had talked so glowingly of it during their ride that she was eager to see it.

Around the last curve the house loomed into view and Caren drew in her breath. It was more, so much more, than Marc had told her. It was a house that fit into its surroundings, embracing the woods, becoming part of nature itself. An A-frame, the long sloping roof fell away from the peak and nearly touched the ground on either side, leaving two walls of the house to be constructed totally of glass. Symmetrically, two fieldstone chimneys jutted out of the roof on both ends and a wide, roughly hewn porch graced both the first and second stories. But it was the expanse of glass that caught Caren's eye. Now, with the afternoon sun shining on it, it reflected the beauty of the woods. Golds, reds, oranges, all seemed to become part of the house. And at night, Caren knew, the moon would cut its path across the heavens never escaping the watchful windowpanes.

Caren was silent, breathless.

"I can see you've already fallen in love with it," Marc intoned. "It does that to me each and every time I come here. I find I'm never immune."

"It is beautiful, Marc. You never overstated its charms when you told me about it."

"You wait and see; it will take you at least a

full day to absorb the beauty of the place, of the woods. I find that every time I come here my first few hours of settling in are concentrated within the house. It's almost as though the eye can't perceive the overwhelming contact with nature. Then, almost without warning, it hits you, and it seeps into your pores and becomes a part of you." As he spoke he looked out the windshield, and then his hand reached out and touched Caren's. "I like sharing this with you, Caren. I'm glad I convinced you to come."

Marc toted their suitcases inside, Caren following. Immediately, she liked what she saw. There were hardly any inner walls in Marc's house. One living space flowed uninterrupted into another. The living room was starkly furnished in chrome and glass, adding to the feeling of unlimited space. On the polished oak floor was a white shag area rug that united the low-slung forest-green sofa and white occasional chairs. Here the fireplace was the focal point in the room—tall and wide, completely constructed of gray fieldstone with a dark blue slate added here and there for definition.

From this area flowed the dining area, again furnished in chrome and glass and the white area rug. The table sat near the glass wall and offered an unobstructed view of the woodlands. Caren noted there were sliding doors that led out onto the deck for dining outdoors.

In the kitchen, the heart of every home, polished birch cabinets complemented pale butcher-block counters and the accent pieces were in oranges and yellows. Even the refrigerator was enameled in citrus yellow, giving life and cheer. Behind the kitchen, just down the hall, was a doorway that led into the bathroom.

Caren had never seen anything like it outside of magazines. One wall was completely glass and silk shades were attached to the tile floor so that the shades could be pulled up for privacy and still allow the sunshine in. The huge circular bathtub, Caren blushingly realized, was large enough for two people, and the area surrounding it was carpeted in plush melon with accents of turquoise, the color of the pillows strewn around the room. The fixtures were a pale beige and from the gleam of the faucets, Caren wondered if they were gold plated.

Here, too, were sliding doors out to a deck, no doubt for sunbathing. But closer examination revealed a California hot tub. Again Caren felt the blood rising to her cheeks. The total effect of the house was contrived to commune with nature and in that very fact, it was also totally sensual.

"We should have everything we need here," Marc called to her from the kitchen, "but if not, there's a store about three miles away. Have you been up to the loft yet?"

"No, where is it?" Caren realized she hadn't seen any sleeping quarters. They must be in the loft.

"Out here, up the stairs. Take a look and pick out your bed."

Caren retraced her steps and found the open-tread staircase leading to the top of the house. The loft was just that, surrounding the downstairs on four sides. The railings were waist high and constructed of rough beams. The floor was thickly carpeted, wall to wall, in a heavenly light blue. She frowned when she saw several low beds covered with patchwork quilts, spaced at intervals around the loft. Then she saw the drop blinds separating one area from another, offering privacy.

"It's all open because it conserves heat and it's efficient to air-condition in the summer." Caren was startled; Marc's voice was so close, right behind her. He reached out and wrapped an arm around her. "How do you like my house, Caren?"

"I love it, Marc, I really do." A thought occurred to her. The house was so much like Marc himself. Open, eye on the world, casually elegant. "You designed it yourself, didn't you?"

"You've guessed." He smiled. "Mind telling me how?"

"It's like you."

"You love my house, Caren. Does that mean you love me, too?" The crinkles at the corners of his eyes deepened. His voice was low, seductive, and suddenly Caren was uncomfortable being here alone with him, sharing this intimacy. Or was he just testing her? Trying to get her to commit herself, to make a fool of herself—or worse, to admit to an emotion and then make her prove it by allowing him to seduce her.

"Loving a house isn't the same as loving a man," she stated simply, moving out of his embrace, heading for the stairs.

"Hold on, you haven't told me which bed you've chosen."

"Where's your bed?" she asked.

"Over there, near the windows." He smiled invitingly.

"Then that's mine, over there." She pointed clear across the loft to a bed near the corner.

Her shoulders were squared, her tone was brittle.

"Take it easy, Caren. Don't get so defensive. You came up here to relax and I'm not in the habit of forcing myself upon unwilling maidens. Now come on, I've got something especially spectacular to show you."

Marc led her down the stairs and out the door. The path led through the woods and the smell of autumn was thick in the air. Dappled shadows created little havens of dimness from the glare of the sun, and arbors were formed by the overhanging branches. They walked side by side, each feeling comfortable in the other's presence. When Marc took her hand in his, she liked the feel of his long, artistic fingers against her own.

Deeper into the woods they walked, stopping to pick an exceptional leaf and stooping to inspect deer tracks. After ten minutes or so, the woods broke into a clearing where the sun was in full reign. And in the center of the clearing was a pond, green and still, reflecting the glory of the sky.

A touch on Caren's cheek brought her attention to Marc. He was lying beside her, watching her, his hand pressing now on the back of her neck, pulling her face down to his.

His kiss was gentle, light and feathery, insisting on little more than this brief contact. She felt herself yielding to him, allowing his lips to part hers, welcoming the intimate pressure. And then his arms were around her, holding her, pressing the length of her body against his own.

The warmth of the sun was on her back, but the fires between their bodies were hotter, consuming. Caren responded, answering his demand, creating demands of her own. Her lips trailed a pattern across his cheek, finding the place where his strong jutting jaw joined his neck. Her hands were in his thick, dark hair, tangling in it, running it through her fingers. All dimension of time was lost. There were only two in this world of reds and golds. Two people, alone, together.

In his embrace, she felt the hard, supple muscles of his arms. Her fingers traced along the wide, strong expanse of his chest; she felt his muscles ripple beneath her touch. His jacket was open; the warmth from him dispelled the chill air. The heady scent of his maleness was heightened by the cool, crisp autumn day. Their legs tangled, their hands sought to know each other, and always, their lips touched.

He pushed her backward, following, bending over her, molding her body to his. His mouth sought the pulse point at the base of her throat and lower, further, down between her breasts, igniting fires, dashing fears. Caren's arms held him, receiving him, offered herself to him.

With a barely audible groan, Marc lifted himself from her. His eyes were dark with unquenched passions, his mouth tight and grim. "Caren," he whispered, "you'll never know how lovely you are. You'll never know how much I want you."

Her eyes held his, dreamy, half closed, like a doe's, in bashful surrender. Her lips, full and passion bruised, were slightly parted. Her hair tumbled about her head, coloring the forest floor with its brightness. Tenderly, his fingers traced a path from her cheek to her lips, touching them lightly, like a kiss. She shivered, trembling from unappeased passion and unquenched desire. No one, ever before, had aroused these feelings in her. No one, not ever, had made her lose control this way. Hot color flushed her cheeks. She had been absolutely brazen in her responses, practically wanton in her desires. Yet from the way

Marc was smiling down into her upturned face, these qualities pleased him, aroused him. Why then did he stop?

"Come on, it's getting late and will be dark soon. We've got to get back to the house." Pulling himself to his feet, he grabbed her hand and helped her up beside him.

Eight

After a dinner of steaks, done on the indoor smokeless grill; fried potatoes, from which Caren abstained; and a crisp green salad, Marc and Caren washed dishes together. Night had fallen blackly, the surrounding woods yielding no light from the moon. The expanse of glass became dark mirrors against the darkness outside. But when Marc moved to the panel beside the front door and flipped a switch, outside spotlights flashed on, bringing the forest to life once again, creating murals of color and dimension as a backdrop.

The living-room fireplace roared to life and warmth with a brightly glowing fire and the built-in stereo system throbbed to Rimski-Korsakov's "Scheherazade." The thick white carpet felt good against their bare feet as they sat on the floor and leaned back against the sofa, sipping at icy glasses of Amaretto.

Peace prevailed as they basked in one another's company, sharing small talk, and light-
hearted humor. The fire shone in Marc's eyes,
softening the chiseled lines in his face, flushing
his cheeks to bronze. Caren settled back beside
him, listening to the music, feeling it pulse
through her, knowing it was Marc's nearness
that quickened her heartbeat, not the symphony.

Marc refilled their glasses, the sweet liqueur
cold and fiery against their lips. When he took
his place beside her he draped his arm over her
shoulder, drawing her closer, resting her head
against his shoulder. After a moment, Caren realized he was looking at her, staring down at her,
as though trying to memorize each and every
line of her face. And when his mouth sought
hers it was with a barely concealed passion.
There was no attempt at tenderness as his lips
ravished hers.

The music surged to a crescendo, rising with
their passion, swelling with intensity. His trac-
ings on her mouth were eloquent expressions of
desire; her responses were stirring burning emotions. Locked in an embrace their longings were
deep and spirited, sharing, giving, taking....

A sharp, heavy rapping sounded on the glass.
At first they thought they imagined the intrusion,

but the knocking continued. With a low, muttered curse, Marc drew away from her, seeking the source of this invasion.

"Marc, Marc, what are you doing in there? Marc! It's me, Moira! Is that girl in there with you?"

Caren's heart sank. Moira, again.

"Marc, do you hear me? I've got to see you! Marc!"

Opening the door, Marc admitted his assistant. "For crying out loud, Moira, how do you manage to find me? You must make it your life's work! What do you want?"

"Marc, is it my fault you refuse to have a phone here in the outback? Remote isn't quite the word for this place, 'isolated' and 'in the sticks' fit it much better." The tall, slim woman entered the living room and spied Caren sitting on the floor opposite the fireplace. "Actually, I've come for our little Miss Ainsley. Somehow some of those preliminary photos have been ruined. We'll have to reshoot them. A good thing we've two days left before she has to leave for Texas."

Caren's spirits sank. Standing, placing her glass on the coffee table, she faced the intruder. "I've given notice that I refuse to be disturbed until it's time to leave for Texas. I can't see how important a few photos are. Mr. Valenti must have thousands.''

''That's just it, darling. Bill Valenti doesn't. They've been sent on to most of the places where you'll be doing personal appearances and shooting on location. These photos are special, black and white, for newspapers and magazines.'' Turning to Marc, she held her hands out in supplication. ''Marc, you know we can't possibly use color photos for newspapers. They won't accept them, they don't show up in print. As for the magazine advertisements—'' She shrugged.

Marc looked at Caren and seemed to deliberate. ''She's right, Caren. We must have those black-and-whites and they can't successfully be made from color prints.''

Caren drew in her breath, ready to do battle. ''But Marc, you promised me these few days—'' Her gaze fell on Moira's smirking face. She'd be willing to bet that those photos were destroyed for the same reason that Jacques had been instructed to sabotage her makeup—the same reason reporters at the preview got word that she was the Nightstar girl.

Caren looked again to Marc. Her heart fell.

She could see he didn't want her to go back to the city to have the pictures taken.

"You had better get your things, Caren," Marc said tonelessly, his eyes never leaving her face.

All the way back to the city, Caren sat between Moira and Marc in the chauffeured limousine, silent. Over and over she thought of her day. It had been idyllic. Dinner had been an easy time together, quiet and friendly. Why did Moira have to ruin everything? Why?

Moira's eyes were on her, watchful, glaringly triumphant.

Caren blinked back tears, refusing to shed them in front of Marc's assistant. Her teeth bit into her lips to keep them from trembling. She leaned back against the seat, wishing she were somewhere, anywhere but here, under Moira's smug gaze. She sighed. Gone were her three days off. Instead she would be facing the camera again. And worse yet, facing an ovenful of dirty dishes.

The welcome Caren received in Texas was worthy of royalty. Everything and everyone was at her beck and call. In her entourage traveled

Jacques, Henri, and Bill Valenti. As a special surprise to Caren, because of her agreement to continue with the promotion and location tour on schedule, Marc Rayven had asked Maggie Bryant to accompany her as her companion. Everything was perfect, or should have been.

Maggie was a wonder. Her natural sense of orderliness helped Caren to arrive at appointments promptly, and aside from her professional help, Maggie was Caren's friend. She had never thought that she would be able to travel, to see the sights and meet all the glamorous people, especially not at company expense; however, because she was a widow, Maggie Bryant was free to travel. She had never had children, so her maternal instincts were focused on Caren.

As Caren lounged for a precious few minutes on the king-size bed in her elegant hotel suite, she scolded herself. I should be counting my blessings! The second half of the tour had been redesigned to include faraway places, foreign countries. Traveling to exotic lands was part of the American dream and Rayven Cosmetics wanted to capitalize on that dream. It had been surveyed as the American woman's fantasy and Marc was now making Nightstar an integral addition to that daydream. Here I am, she sighed, in a position most girls would envy, surrounded by friends and people who only wish the best for me, and instead I sit here fighting back tears. Why? Why?

The answer was disgustingly evident—Marc Rayven. Marc had been in touch with his production manager daily. He had even had conversations with Jacques and Henri after seeing the daily rushes that were messengered to him in New York by express. Even Maggie had been called to the phone to talk to the makeup mogul, but never Caren. She was the ignored member of the wandering tribe.

The personal-appearance tour, combined with location photography sessions, had begun in Texas. From there it had traveled to Los Angeles and San Francisco. But never, never a word from Marc Rayven.

She suspected he had been behind some of the ideas the production manager had created for the commercials. Clothing was being expressed to her from some of the most famous designers. From what Caren could gather, many designers were begging Marc to allow them to create something for Caren to wear on camera. There was the linen suit from Halston; she had worn it in Los Angeles, at the filming in front of the

Chinese Theatre; and at the Hollywood Bowl, she had posed in a Givenchy dream. San Francisco had demanded a Bill Blass silk classic as she wandered the hills. But always Bill Valenti's camera had caught her looking romantic and wistful.

Now here she was in Chicago with her little entourage and something was dreadfully wrong. Aside from the bitterness she was feeling concerning Marc Rayven and his beautiful and sophisticated assistant, something was going wrong with the shooting.

Bill Valenti was constantly in conference with Jacques and Henri, prodding them to try new makeup, new hairstyles. And still he wasn't happy with the results. Only an hour before, Jacques had come to Caren's room to talk with her.

The Frenchman had begun by telling her he considered himself her "Dutch Uncle." "Caren, I want you to feel you can talk to me. Something is eating at you and it's showing on camera. There's a coldness about you, a defen- siveness, that wasn't there when we first began."

"I don't know what you mean, Jacques," she had answered honestly, not understanding what the Frenchman meant.

"I don't know either, Caren. You're still as sweet and charming as when I first met you, yet something is coming across on camera—"

Giving his typical Frenchman's shrug, he peered deeply at her. "*Chérie,* there are little lines of discontent and unhappiness that even the most artfully applied makeup cannot hide. May I be personal and ask if you are having problems in your love life?"

Caren laughed harshly. "What love life, Jacques? You never see anyone hanging around, do you? Really, I can't imagine what you're talking about. I try my best, it seems I'll have to try harder—"

"No, no, *chérie.* Trying harder is not the answer for that special look.... Ah, I'm being a foolish old man."

Now, stretched out on the satin coverlet on her lonely bed, Caren remembered the exchange and forced it out of her mind. Trying harder was the answer; she knew it, it had to be. She'd try to take better care of herself. Eat more, for one thing. She didn't like the gaunt look that was unbecoming to her. And for another, she'd try to rest more. How could a girl look romantic when she was dead on her feet?

As she glanced at her bedside clock, the ringing phone startled her. Seven o'clock. It must be Maggie calling to have dinner with her. But it wasn't Maggie's voice on the other end of the line.

"Caren? Marc here."

Marc! Oh, how she begrudged the lifting and soaring that took place in her heart just from hearing his voice. Hang on tight, she warned herself. He's probably calling to tell you how disappointed he's been in the daily rushes. "Hello, Mr. Rayven," she said simply, breath bated for what he would say.

"Have you had dinner yet?" His tone was casual, friendly, and close, so close she could have sworn he was calling from the next room.

"No...no, I haven't eaten yet. I was waiting for Maggie—"

"Maggie's having dinner with Bill Valenti and the rest of the crew. What about yourself?"

Now how did he know who Maggie was having dinner with? "I—I guess I'll have room service send something up...Mr. Rayven. Why are you calling me?"

"To have dinner, of course. I'm here in Chicago, right down the hall from you, as a matter of fact."

Down the hall! Her heart beat like a triphammer, thudding and thudding against her ribs, taking her breath away. Her tongue stuck to the roof of her mouth; words refused to come. She wanted to tell him she loved him…. No! No! She wanted to tell him to stay away, that she couldn't see him, that she was too tired. Instead, her silence committed her.

"Fine," Marc was saying, taking command as always. "I'll pick you up in a half hour. Unless, of course, you want to stick to your original plan. We could have dinner in your room—or mine, if you prefer."

Dinner? Here in this room, alone with him? No…no…

"I'll be ready in half an hour," she managed to sputter. No matter how tired she was, she'd drag herself out. If she must see him, it would be outside this room, where there were people, where she could defend herself against him.

Exactly one-half hour later a knock sounded on her door. A quick glance in the mirror at her Bill Blass silk suit and casual, free-flowing hairdo told her she was looking her best. After all, if it was good enough for the Nightstar commercial, it was good enough for dinner with Marc Rayven. She had already decided she wouldn't invite him into her room, and she had bathed and dressed in record time. She had actually been waiting for him for three whole minutes!

Picking up her slim handbag, she went to the door and opened it. There stood Marc and his good looks almost took her breath away. How was it that she hadn't remembered how handsome he was? Somehow, Caren felt she was losing her grip on things. In a disconcerted manner she flashed him an automatic smile and closed the door to her suite behind her. Darn, she hoped she had remembered to put her room key in her handbag. Well, she wasn't going to check for it now, not with Marc's glistening blue eyes watching her. That was a problem she would have to deal with later.

"You're lovely, Caren, as always. It's so good to see you again. Have you missed me?" His tone was soft, casual, intimate.

Of all the nerve, she thought, still smiling. He could have told her that *he'd* missed *her!* She parried his question. "Actually, I've got this boss who keeps me fairly busy," she said lightly, avoiding his eyes.

"Ummm. You're wearing Nightstar. You delight me—"

"What would you expect me to wear?" she

answered caustically. "You did hire me to promote your product and that's what I do."

Marc seemed taken aback by her remark, but he quickly recovered. "Where would you like to have dinner? I'm a key member of the Playboy Club. Chicago is their national headquarters, you know. Or perhaps you'd enjoy something else?"

Playboy Club, indeed. How fitting, she thought nastily. There was no way she was going to sit through dinner and watch Marc ogle all those little bunnies. And some not so little, she thought as she glanced down at her own modest bosom. "I've heard so many nice things about Benihanas. It's not too far from here."

"Japanese food it is," he agreed, taking her arm and leading her to the elevators. "But I'll have to watch myself. Because of your hostility I'm afraid you'll take one of those cleavers the cooks use and bury it in my skull."

Caren laughed, a rousing, sincere laugh. Things were going to be fine. She just knew it.

Outside, the streets were decorated for the coming holidays. Red Santas and silver stars lined the streets, illuminated with power from the streetlamps. There was an air of Christmas and peace on earth in the lovely city. The wind off the lake was brisk and invigorating but not frigid or gusty. There was a calm permeating the atmosphere and it seemed to filter into Caren as well.

"Do you love Christmas?" he asked her. "You seem to be the kind of girl who does. Does your family mind it that you won't be with them this year?"

Caren shook her head. "No, there's really no family any longer. Mom and Dad are gone and I've sort of lost touch with aunts and uncles. But Christmas makes me feel all warm inside anyway. I remember the traditions my grandmother used to follow and then my own mother did the same. I try to keep them myself. Sometimes there doesn't seem much point—but I try."

"You always give everything your best shot, don't you?" Marc asked respectfully.

"I try!" Caren giggled, lengthening her stride to match his.

As they rounded a corner onto Michigan Boulevard, they found themselves in front of the John Hancock skyscraper. "Have you had time to go to the top of 'Big John'?" Caren shook her head. "Well, now's as good a time as any. I've never been either—" He quickened his steps, carrying her along with him, making her breathless.

The long elevator ride to the top of the sky-scraper had its usual effect on her, and she felt as though her stomach had swung from her throat to her toes and had settled somewhere off kilter. She followed Marc out of the elevator and down the hall into the bar whose panoramic windows revealed the city below in all its glory.

As they stood near the glass, Caren could feel the building being buffeted by the winds off the lake; the sheer drop to the city below was frightening. But standing here with Marc, with his arm draped casually around her waist, she had never felt so safe and secure in all her life. Below they could see the bright red and green lights of Christmas decorations. Out on the lake marinas and small boats were lit, creating a string of glistening gems against the black waters. And the sky! Tonight the sky was clear and every star, millions of them, shone brightly in the special way they do in the winter sky.

No words were exchanged between them. No words were needed. The excitement and beauty of the city came alive for them in each other's presence. It was shared and cherished, a sight never to be forgotten.

"Caren, how would you like to have dinner here? I could make a reservation right now, and we could look at the city and watch the stars. Perhaps we could even find that nightstar you told me about at that first board meeting. Would you like that?''

Her smile was his answer.

Dinner was perfect, the service sublime and unobtrusive. Throughout the meal Marc told her of his boyhood, and they exchanged silly stories about when they were children. No mention of the company was made, no reference to the Nightstar campaign spoiled their celebratory mood.

It was with great reluctance that they stepped into the elevator and descended to street level. The wind had kicked up quite a bit so they ran back to the hotel, skipping down the street like children. Their cheeks were rosy and their toes were frozen by the time they arrived, to the amused glances of the doorman and the desk clerk.

In the lobby Marc pulled her over to the main desk and picked up the house phone. ''Hot buttered rum for two. Room 1132. And make it quick.''

It was a full minute before she realized that Marc had ordered the hot beverage for two! And in *her* room!

"You like hot toddies, don't you?" he asked as they stepped into the elevator.

"Huh?" She hadn't heard him, so engrossed in her thoughts was she.

"I asked you—" His arms came around her, softly, tenderly, pulling her against him, close, so close she could feel his breath upon her cheek. "Who do you love, Caren? Tell me, who do you love?"

Her answer was in her eyes, but she knew he couldn't see it because her eyes had closed as his mouth covered hers, possessing it, adoring it. When he released her, it was just as the elevator door opened and a man entered. Blushing, Caren lowered her head and waited for the lift to stop at the eleventh floor. They ran from the elevator, laughing and giggling at being caught in an embrace. Lightheartedly, Marc challenged her to a race down the hall and courteously allowed her to win.

Still laughing and breathless, she fumbled in her handbag for the key and waited while Marc opened the door.

"You really should leave," she told him after he had tuned in the radio to an all-music station. "I do have my job to consider and you know I have to look my best."

"Oh yes, your job. I'm not sure they'll be shooting tomorrow. Valenti told me he was going to scout the city for a backdrop to shoot against. His assistants haven't come up with much, it seems."

"Marc, how about the top of the John Hancock building. It was beautiful there—"

"No." His answer was abrupt, almost stern.

"I—I just thought—"

"No," he told her as he gathered her in his arms. "That's our place. We discovered it together and I don't want it run in a commercial to promote some perfume. Tonight was too special—too perfect. Understand?"

Caren nodded, falling against him, offering her lips and also her heart.

Room service knocked and Marc ushered the waiter into the room. The buttered rum was soothing, warming after the cold Chicago weather. Room service had added an assortment of cheese straws and like greedy children they consumed them, and brushed the cracker crumbs off Caren's bed where they sat.

"What would you like to do tomorrow? We have the whole day."

"Tomorrow? But I thought you had to return

to New York, and Maggie and I promised each
other a shopping trip at the Water Tower Place.''

The pleading look in his eyes persuaded her
that there were more urgent needs to be filled.

''Can't you go with me instead of Maggie?
Maggie will have you for the rest of the tour.
We could do some Christmas shopping. I will
need your expert advice, you know. There's the
production crew, Maggie, Jacques, and Henri....
Say you will,'' he demanded, touching her neck
just below her ear with his lips, nibbling softly,
persuading.

''I'll call Maggie in the morning—''

Again she was swept into his arms. Again her
world spun and tilted.

The next day was a blustery day of winter.
Marc called for her at eleven and instructed her
to wear slacks and dress warmly. Bundled into
gray wool slacks with a bright red pullover,
Caren slipped into the white rabbit coat that had
been made for her as part of her campaign wardrobe. ''You look terrific,'' Maggie complimented Caren as she searched for a pair of
woolen gloves. ''But you'll freeze if you wear
those skimpy kidskin gloves. This is Chicago,

Caren, and it's a whole lot closer to the North Pole than it appears on the map.''

Caren laughed, excitement bubbling out of her. She found she was laughing quite a bit since Marc had taken her out the night before. Or was that just because there had been so little to make her happy until he arrived on the scene?

"Maggie, you're a wonder not to mind about me going shopping with Marc.''

"Don't be silly,'' Maggie assured her. "I do most of my shopping for Christmas throughout the year. You know how it is, picking up little bargains on a typist's salary. Besides, I'm saving my money for when we go on tour. I love shopping in new stores and boutiques. I plan to return home with a king's ransom.''

The tour...new cities...new shops and glittering boutiques... How could Caren have forgotten? She would be on location at Christmas time. And Marc would be in New York, no doubt. In New York with Moira over the holiday season. Suddenly crestfallen, Caren slumped down on the edge of the bed.

"What's the matter, honey? What's gotten into you? Aren't you feeling well?'' Maggie asked solicitously, touching her fingertips to Caren's forehead.

"I'm fine, Maggie. Just a little homesick, I guess. To me Christmas means glitter and polish and snow and turkey and there won't be any of that where we're going. What I mean is it will be there, but it won't be the same as back home."

Maggie clucked and crooned, holding Caren in her arms. "To me Christmas means being with someone special. Someone who means more to you than anyone else in the world." She sighed so deeply that Caren pulled away and stared at her. Could it be possible that Maggie did have someone special and she had given that up to accompany Caren on the tour?

"Who's your someone special, Maggie? Anyone I know?"

"No, you wouldn't know him. I met him back in New York and we became very close. I'll miss him, but then I won't be all alone as he will. I'll have you and Bill and Jacques and Henri. My someone special is from England and all his family is there. Business reasons are keeping him in New York."

"Oh, Maggie, that's terrible! I don't want you to go on tour with me. I want you to go back to New York—"

"Don't be silly. The arrangements have all

been made. Besides, Mr. Rayven is counting on me and I won't let him down.'' Maggie's voice was adamant. She would not tolerate an argument. Period.

There was no time for further discussion. Just as Maggie found Caren's bright red woolen gloves, Marc announced himself at the door. Breezing out to warnings to keep buttoned up, Caren literally danced out of the suite and down the hall; the only thing keeping her feet on the ground was the steadying influence of Marc's hand in hers.

The day was colder than either Marc or Maggie had predicted, but Caren reveled in it. The new Water Tower Place shopping mall was only blocks away from the Hancock skyscraper and Caren insisted they walk. They decided that after the shopping mall they would continue down Michigan Boulevard to the numerous art galleries and antique shops. Surely something appropriate could be found in one of those places for the very particular Jacques.

Inside the seven-storied shopping mall, Christmas carols jubilantly rang out. People scurried from one store to another, jostling each other in a friendly manner and smiling, always smiling. The season was upon them and in their hearts.

At a jewelry store a gold cigarette case was purchased for Jacques. Caren, who could not afford anything so extravagant, settled on a pair of jade cuff links for Henri.

For Maggie, Caren found a simple gold chain from which was suspended a tiny gold three-dimensional box containing a mustard-seed grain for good luck. Marc added to Maggie's Christmas present by purchasing a slim gold watch, which was neat and tailored, just like Maggie herself.

At a leather-goods store Marc bought an English cowhide wallet for Bill Valenti and an exquisite attaché case for Henri in which he could carry all the tools of his trade.

The silversmith carried the perfect gifts for Caren to purchase for Jacques: an engraved mustache cup and a sterling money clip. For Bill Valenti, Caren spied a Norman Rockwell lithograph she just knew the photographer would like.

"Time for lunch, Caren," Marc said with authority. "My arms are breaking and I thought Santa Claus carried his own bag of goodies."

Marc led the way to an old English pub he

had seen on the third level. The Black Bull offered a delectable menu of luncheon entrées and they decided on thinly sliced beef and a crisp green salad.

As they were leaving, their pert blonde waitress pointedly studied Caren. Suddenly, recognition dawned upon her. "You're Caren Ainsley, the Nightstar girl, aren't you? I've asked my husband for a bottle of Nightstar for Christmas." The waitress' glance went to Marc and then back to Caren. "Now I'll know who put those stars in your eyes when I see you in magazines and on TV. I have to admit, those commercials are the most romantic advertising I've ever seen, and you're wonderful in them."

Caren's voice, when she spoke, was hesitant. "Thank...thank you. How nice of you to say so."

The blonde laughed and waved them a goodbye and a happy holiday. Outside the pub in the midst of the holiday shopping Marc pressed close up against Caren. "Am I?"

"Are you what?"

"Am I the reason you have stars in your eyes? Tell me," he whispered. "I want to hear you say it."

All around them people milled; strangers'

eyes glanced at them speculatively. Not even before the cameras or on nationwide television had Caren felt so conspicuous and exposed. Marc held her fast, demanding that she tell him. Again, he repeated, "Tell me, Caren. Is it true? Am I the reason you have stars in your eyes?"

Color crept into Caren's face and Marc tipped up her chin, peering down at her. "That's all I wanted to know," he said huskily before covering her mouth with his own and making her oblivious to the fact that people were passing by and staring.

The next day Marc had to leave to go back to New York and he took Maggie Bryant with him at Caren's request. Just because she, Caren, was going to be away from the man she loved at Christmas, was no reason for Maggie to be away from the city and the friends she loved.

The crew finished up in Chicago and Bill Valenti and Jacques seemed especially pleased with the results of the shooting. Three days' shooting in Atlanta, Georgia, and another five days in the Caribbean.

Each day Marc called her, sometimes twice a day. Bill seemed ecstatic with her performance before the cameras, and Jacques wore a grin that said it all.

The plan was to leave for the Nevada desert the following morning. All the details had been handled by Marc personally. It was to be the next-to-last location before returning to New York to await the results of the first half of the campaign. A month or so for rest and relaxation and then they would tackle the foreign market with a lengthy tour. How excited Marc had been with his idea for the Nevada desert. He said it was a preview of things to come. His description of the Arabian hotel in the middle of the desert had made her breathless. Half old world and half new world. They would stay in the old part of the hotel with all the Eastern flavor and culture the owner refused to change.

"You'll think you're really in the Arabian desert, Caren," Marc had said with enthusiasm. "Even the shopping plaza was designed to resemble a mock Arabian bazaar. You're going to love it!" If he said she was going to love it she knew she would. Imagine someone with enough money to build an Arabian palace in the middle of the Nevada desert. She grinned when she recalled Marc's saying that commercialism had won out and the owner had been forced to add onto the palace—a more modern building that American guests desired.

The phone near her bed rang and Caren quickly snatched it up. It was Marc. It was always Marc. This time his voice was excited.

"I've done it! I've cleared my desk. I'll be joining you in Nevada for Christmas after all. Tell me you can't wait to see me."

It was a dream come true. Marc. Marc would meet her in Nevada. He was going to spend Christmas with her. "I can't wait," she bubbled happily into the phone. "Hurry," she whispered before she replaced the phone in its cradle.

Nine

Caren blinked. Impossible was the only word that came to mind. How had Marc Rayven's crew made all this possible? It was a world apart from anything she had ever seen. It was unbelievable, but Eastern sights and sounds assaulted her senses. The costumes, the settings in the desert, were all ancient world. Harem pants, brocaded vests, glittering face veils, and pillows were everywhere. Hundreds of them, thousands of them, surrounded her. It was a make-believe world, compliments of Rayven Cosmetics and the expertise of Jacques, Bill, and many others.

Silken tents were constructed on the desert. There were even a few camels and goatherds to fill the background. Who had gotten them and from where were complete mysteries to Caren. Make-believe bazaars and temples were used as backdrops. And always, Marc sat on his stool just behind the camera, watching. Scenes were created in rapid-fire succession. Bill Valenti seemed very pleased with her work. Daily rushes were viewed and notes were taken on their editing. The world was a beautiful place; the work went well. And always, there was Marc—taking her around to see the sights and to give her a personal tour of the old palace-motel in the desert, taking her to dinners and pageants and to the real bazaar for endless shopping tours.

Caren knew she had never been so happy in her life and that happiness was Marc Rayven. But an icy wind blew across the desert late one afternoon when Moira Evans suddenly arrived. Caren's world seemed to crash down around her when Moira favored her with a deadly look. That one look told Caren that whatever excuse Moira had used to bring herself to Nevada was either trumped up or created especially for this purpose. The president's beautiful assistant was here to protect her territory—and that territory was labeled "Marc Rayven."

Dusk, her favorite time of day. Aimlessly, Caren strolled along the wide balcony of her hotel suite. This was her time, her private time of day to sit and contemplate the day's happenings. A time to relax, a time to ponder, and a time to make decisions. Gripping the balcony rail like a vise, she stared into the pearl-gray shadows of early evening. "I love Marc Rayven," she said to the stillness around her.

This stop in the Nevada desert was the next to last in the ad campaign. When they finished shooting here on location, they would head for home to wait out the results of this first half of the tour.

If only she could be sure of Marc's feelings for her. True, he had kissed her as a man kisses the woman he loves, and true, he had murmured all the right words in response to her own husky whispers. Yet, he had said nothing that could be taken as a commitment. He had made no promise of what would be when the Nightstar campaign was over. And there was Moira Evans always lurking within eyesight and earshot.

Caren's eyes narrowed as she stared down into the courtyard beneath the balcony. The early twilight wove lacy patterns over ancient, gnarled trees that circled the small area. Marc! Moira! Unable to tear her eyes from the couple, Caren stared, willing her eyes to see clearly in the semidarkness. She shivered slightly in the evening air. What were they saying to each other? As she watched the couple, the lavender shadows deepened and lengthened, cloaking the small private garden in soft, caressing blackness. She was frightened.

Suddenly, the garden was bathed in a dim, yellowish glow from the apartments beneath her own. The silhouettes standing under the tree leaned toward each other and seemed to melt into oneness. Caren gasped and felt as though her heart were being ripped to shreds. It was a long embrace, each second doing more damage to her wounded heart. Then Moira's words, clear and distinct, wafted toward her in the cool evening, making her wish for a chasm to fall into.

Caren raced back into her apartment as though a devil chased at her heels. It was a game. It had been a game all along. Marc was playing a game to get what he wanted—and she was the loser. The cool, mocking words had seared her brain, penetrated her being. ''You've succeeded, Marc. As Jacques said, the only thing missing was the 'look of love.' Now that you've succeeded in making Caren fall in love with you, you're going to have to come up with a way to extricate yourself gracefully. Little girls like Caren can be crushed so easily. Better to bruise her now than later since she thinks that all of this was serious on your part, Marc. We only have three days here and then home to New York. Start to wean her away from you now. She has to realize sooner or later that it was a trick. In time she'll forget about it—as the residuals come in from the commercials. Money, plenty of it, can work wonders. And to think we have you and Jacques to thank for making this the perfect campaign. I still can't believe that he was astute enough to come up with the idea that what was missing in Caren's eyes was the 'look of love,' or that you were magnanimous enough to cast aside your own feelings to make the little pigeon fall in love with you. I, for one, call that dedication above and beyond the call of duty. I understand better than anyone how far you'll go to make this company the number-one cosmetics firm in the country.''

Silence. Caren sobbed into the scarlet pillow on the chaise. She shouldn't have stood there and listened; she hoped Marc and Moira were enjoying the little trick they had pulled on poor, unsuspecting Caren. How could they...how could he have done this to her? He certainly knew how naive she was.

Caren jumped up from the chaise and recklessly started to toss her clothing into the stack of suitcases with which she traveled. She gave no thought to wrinkles or the havoc she was creating. Shoes were dumped unceremoniously on top of sheer blouses, and tailored slacks found themselves tangled up with gossamer nighties. Her eye fell on a cut-glass decanter with the silver-and-gold medallion that represented the Nightstar perfume. Without a second thought she picked it up and threw it against the mosaic tiles on the floor. Minuscule shards of crystal flew into the air as the heady scent permeated the room. She stared at the sparkling slivers of glass as they settled on the tiles. Shattered, just as she was. It was over. In a split second she had destroyed Marc Rayven's perfume just as Moira's words had destroyed her.

She had to get out of here, out of this room, away from the heavy, cloying scent that was everywhere, making it impossible to breathe. The cool evening air would help her to get her thoughts together. Run, her mind shrieked. Run fast and hard and don't think. Without a backward glance, Caren flung open the door and raced down the corridor and then down the stairwell.

Everything smelled like the perfume that was soaking into the tiles in her room. It seemed to be all about her, in her hair, in her nostrils, in her mouth, and on her clothes. "I hate it, I hate it,'' she choked out over and over as she ran around the building into a formal garden. Then, she slowed down, picking her way carefully between the lush foliage.

She roamed the gardens from end to end for what seemed like hours, until, drying her tears on the hem of the colorful caftan she wore, Caren looked at her surroundings to see how far she had come. Tiny, twinkling lights from the hotel to the east told her she had come much farther than she intended. She was going to have a long walk back. Strangely enough, no thoughts for her safety entered her head. It seemed a peaceful, quiet place. She walked a short distance and sat down on a tile bench beneath a monstrous old tree.

Peaceful and sad, her tears dried, Caren kept up a running conversation with herself. ''Am I sad for what was, what is, or what is not to be?'' She could find no answers to her silent questions. Wearily, she rose and gathered the material of the caftan in her hand. Daintily, she picked her way through the garden. When something was over, it was over. You went on from there.

Tears pricked at her eyes as she continued to walk in the direction of the hotel. She gulped and swallowed hard. No more tears. The time for tears was over. Now it was time to be angry, gut angry for having been made a fool. How could he! No, that was wrong. How dare he!

Mentally, Caren ticked off the appointments on her schedule for the following day and the day after that. If she was careful, she could almost manage to stay away from Marc. Her free time would be taken up with complaints: it was too hot; she had a headache; the water was getting to her; she had stomachaches from the spicy food.

The lights from the hotel were closer now, just beyond the circle of trees that flanked the formal gardens. How strange this majestic hotel looked sitting here in the desert, half old world and half concrete and steel.

For a moment Caren was disoriented as she took in her surroundings. Now she appeared to be on the side of the original hotel, palace really—the west side. A glance at her watch told her a good three and a half hours had passed since she had stormed out of the hotel. She had missed dinner, and, of course, the inevitable cocktails beforehand with Moira, Jacques, and Marc. What had they thought when she hadn't shown up in the dining room? Marc had probably sent Moira to her room, and by now she would have reported the smashed bottle of scent and the disarray of the half-packed luggage. Caren turned, closing the iron gate behind her.

It was another world, a garden within a garden, manicured to perfection. She stopped. Surely, this oasis in the desert wasn't for the guests. Perhaps it belonged to the owners. She stood, puzzled as to what to call the area. It wasn't a room, and yet it wasn't a patio either. She moved closer, each step taking her back in time to the legends and the palaces of ancient Rome. Arcades were fastened along two sides of what looked like a room, and beneath each tiled and marble arch stood braziers that burned brightly to give both light and warmth. Long, low divans upholstered in marvelously rich fabrics lined the two walls. The floor beneath Caren's feet was carpeted in the most lush jewellike colors of the rainbow; these created a translucent effect that made the floor covering appear thicker and more welcoming to the foot. Tapestries, which Caren recognized as coming from French looms, were hung from pedestals supporting figurines and statues of goddesses. The area had a furnished feeling that in no way detracted from the simple sweep of what she was sure was the finest in old-world architecture.

To the left was a pool fed by an outside stream, and floating atop the blue-tinted water were rose petals and fragrant pomanders studded with spices. Upon closer examination, Caren discovered that a pit had been fashioned outside the perimeters of the pool, and within this pit were polished rocks heated by burning fragrant oil. Caren dipped her hand into the clear water and tested its temperature. Pleasantly warm, soothingly so. The continual runoff from the pool emptied itself into a trough that fell beneath the floor and ran to the outside garden. Never in her life had she imagined such luxury. Who had devised the mechanics of it? That person was a genius—a genius in his field as Marc Rayven was in the cosmetics industry. Now the moment was spoiled. She had allowed thoughts of Marc to creep into it. Now the beauty of this special place was shattered, ruined. How could she appreciate it when Marc Rayven was trampling roughshod over her heart and mind?

"So, you found it on your own," a quiet voice near her said.

Startled, Caren whirled and stood staring at

Marc Rayven. Her heart leaped to her throat making it impossible to answer. She nodded.

"I was here many years ago, and when we checked in at the main desk, I specifically asked for this suite of rooms. I think this garden, this small oasis, is about the closest thing to perfection that a man could find. All it needs is a woman to make it complete. Tell me, how do you like it?"

She couldn't have spoken if her life depended on it. She shrugged, aware of his nearness. Carefully, she backed off a step and then another one.

The silence between Marc and Caren continued, each alone with their thoughts, yet ever aware of the other's presence. The air was wine sweet and left Caren lightheaded. Still the silence continued, and when he reached out his hand and captured hers, they walked out into the chill night, hand in hand. Caren filled her lungs with the bracing air and felt a slight, pleasant buzz in her head. She looked up at him as they walked, conscious of his height, his maleness. His hand was warm on hers; her shoulder brushed his arm and tingled with the contact. They walked across the gardens, out onto the grassy knoll. Beneath the cover of the trees, hidden from the stars, they stopped. He took her in his arms and the universe clashed.

She had no will, no desire to stop him. She needed this as much as she needed to take another breath. Tomorrow was another day to make decisions.

His mouth became a part of hers, and her heart beat in a wild, broken rhythm without a pattern. They strained toward each other, caught up in the designs of the flesh as they toiled to join breath and spirit.

They tore at each other, each seeking that which the other could give. There in the shadows of the trees, away from the prying light of the heavens, they devoured each other with their searching lips and hungry fingers.

It was Marc who gently extricated her from the circle of his arms. "Not here, not now," he said huskily.

To her ears the words were tortured, full of something that sounded like regret.

Marc was quiet for so long Caren didn't realize that she had been holding her breath, hardly daring to breathe until he spoke. She let her breath escape in a long sigh.

Marc's voice was carefully controlled, Caren thought. "I suppose what I'm really saying is that things aren't always what they appear to be. Things change, people change.'' Again there was a silence. Caren waited. ''Tricks, for want of a better word, aren't always tricks, per se, like when we were children. From any experience, even betrayal, we learn and we grow.'' His voice was hesitant, less controlled, as if the words he chose were not to his liking.

Again Caren waited, a small knot of fear tightening in her stomach. The words swirled around her head, making her dizzy. They were words; anyone could say words. It was what the words meant that was important. She understood now and the words were his. He was admitting that he had betrayed her. He wasn't going to use her again and make a fool of her—not again.

''Do you understand what I just said?'' Marc said quietly.

Caren stood up and deliberately moved away from the nest Marc had created beneath the tree. ''I understand perfectly, Mr. Rayven. You used me to make a success of your company. You pretended to fall in love with me so that I would come across on camera with the 'look of love.' Well, you succeeded. I did fall in love with you. You boasted that you could turn me into a silk purse and you succeeded. Well, Mr. Rayven, I no longer want to be a silk purse. I like what I was. In fact, Mr. Rayven, I hate you from the top of your head to the bottom of your feet. But you're right about one thing—we do learn from each and every experience. You're nothing but a slick, conniving, dyed-in-the-wool phony. You...you...Lipstick King. Oh, and one last thing, from here on in, Mr. Rayven, you're on your own. I quit.''

Marc's face was in the shadows but his eyes took on the glaze of rage. His fingers bit into her arm, squeezing, hurting. He was frightening her, making her want to run like a rabbit and hide away from him—away from his rage.

''Caren, listen to me!'' It was an order.

She bristled, railing against her traitorous impulses. No, she told herself, no! She had listened enough already and where had it gotten her? To the deserts of Nevada with nothing to show for it but a badly injured ego and a broken heart.

''No!'' she protested, tearing her arm from his grip. ''I've heard enough!''

He seized her again, shaking her till she thought she could hear her teeth rattle. ''If you won't listen to explanations, then you'll listen to this! You have a contract, Miss Ainsley and it is not complete until you finish the next two days' shooting. And finish it you will! Not another word, do you understand?'' he bellowed.

She understood. She understood *everything*.

Caren glanced at the watch that lay next to an empty coffee cup on a stool. Two more hours and her contract was finished. Two more hours and she could pack it in and head for home. How she had gotten through the past forty-two hours was beyond her. Willpower, guts, stamina, call it what you will, she had delivered. And she had paid her dues in full. No one, and that included Marc Rayven, could say she had been anything but professional. She had bent but she hadn't broken under Rayven's steely gaze and sharp tongue. She had more than delivered. Jacques said she was as professional as they come. Henri had said he would be glad to work with her anytime, anyplace. Only Marc Rayven had remained silent, his eyes cold and hard. Now that it was down to the wire with only two more shots to finish one would think he would have the decency to at least congratulate her. Oh no, the perfume wizard was going to get every minute out of her if it killed her. What did he care as long as he made money and his campaign was successful?

"Bill, in the last two shots don't use the handbag. Too awkward." Marc Rayven shouted to be heard over the music that Jacques was playing in the background.

Caren's back stiffened. "Now just a minute, Mr. Rayven. I've done everything you wanted; I've followed orders. But the purse stays or you can get yourself another girl for the last two shots. It's my right," she said heatedly. At his perplexed look at her outburst she rushed on. "If anyone deserves to be photographed with a purse—a *silk* purse—it's me. Take it or leave it," she continued hotly.

Marc Rayven flinched and then stood. "You're absolutely right. Shoot it, and use the silk purse. Somehow, I hadn't thought you would have come so...prepared," he said, letting his eyes come to rest on a square of scarlet silk attached to a thin gold chain.

"That's been the problem all along. You never thought I could think on my own. I meant it when I said I want the purse in the shot," Caren said coolly.

"And I meant it when I told Bill to use the purse." Without another word he left her standing alone, more alone than she had ever been in her entire life.

It was over. Finished. Done. Quickly she gathered her things together and was off and running, her long legs pumping furiously. Her adrenaline flowed as if someone had tapped an underground spring. By the time she reached her apartment and locked the door securely, the phone was ringing. She fixed the black instrument with a steely gaze and shouted, "Ring all night for all I care!" Within minutes she'd finished her haphazard packing. She would leave on the first available plane.

Why did he have to beat around the bush? Why couldn't he just be man enough to come out and say he'd duped her, that he didn't love her and had only been pretending. If he had done that she would at least respect him for his honesty. After all, one person could not make another person love someone.

Her mouth was a grim, tight line as she fished in her bag for her airline ticket. Her hand was on the phone, ready to pick up the receiver, when it shrilled to life. She withdrew her hand as though a snake had lashed out at her. She stared at the ebony instrument with unblinking eyes, willing it to stop its insistent bid for attention. The moment it ceased to ring Caren picked up the phone and asked to be connected with the airport. Thirty-five minutes later she had a con-firmed reservation for the following day at six P.M. It was over. She was going back home to her little two-room apartment. It was time to get on with her life—whatever that was and wher-ever it would lead her. Later, much later, she would decide about the second half of the tour.

A bath. Always take a warm, soothing bath and you will feel better. She had read that some-where. Picking her way over the broken perfume decanter, Caren walked into the bathroom and turned on the gilt faucet. Water rushed into the tub creating a halo of steam that spiraled up-ward. She watched with clinical interest to see if the water pressure would change. Amazing—the torrent of water filled the tub within minutes. The phone shrilled again at the same time a loud rapping occurred at her door. Thank God for the old part of the palace-hotel where the doors were stout and some macho hero couldn't break it down with his manly perfumed shoulders.

When the phone stilled, Caren picked it up for the second time and spoke to the desk clerk. She enunciated slowly and clearly. "I don't want any calls put through to my room this evening." The moment she replaced the receiver, it clamored to life. So much for clear distinct instructions said in a firm, no-nonsense voice.

She felt confused, out of sorts. Where to go, what to do? She could go to the shopping center, the one fashioned like an old-world bazaar. She should have thought of that sooner. She could go there and while away her hours and be lost to anyone from Rayven Cosmetics.

The phone jangled again, jarring her nerves. It was Marc; she knew it. How long would it be before he decided to come pounding on her door? Before she could allow herself to be trapped in her room, forced to see him, hear him, she rushed out the door and slammed it shut behind her.

Caren realized too late that she was still dressed in her bright yellow silk caftan that was more loungewear than outdoor attire. Halfway down the long hallway she remembered that her key was locked in her room behind the door she had just slammed closed.

Too late. She wouldn't go down to the desk and explain so that she could get a spare key because she couldn't run the risk of encountering Marc Rayven. Not ever!

Ten

An hour later Caren trudged into the desert shopping plaza. There were busy shoppers everywhere as she weaved her way among the throngs in the plaza bazaar. Suddenly she realized she was hungry. But she immediately remembered that she had no money with her. She shrugged; her stomach would have to wait. Each stall was more colorful than the next. The Christmas decorations made her feel sentimental as she followed a group of tourists. The smells were entrancing. One stall held every cheese imaginable while the one next to it was decorated with every exotic flower under the sun.

"Peaches! Peaches! Ripe and succulent peaches! Fit for a king! Firm and delicious! Peaches! Peaches!" The merchant held out a plump, pink peach as he stood before Caren. "Ah, lovely lady, see how firm and sweet they are. Their beauty is equaled by your own."

Caren shook her head. She turned her palms up to show she had no money with her.

"For you, lovely lady, it is a gift. Enjoy."

Caren accepted the peach reluctantly and thanked the vendor. She devoured the fruit, the thick, rich juice dribbling down her cheek. "Food fit for a god." She smiled at the merchant. He nodded his head as Caren continued with her progress down the narrow aisle.

Tired from all the walking she was doing, Caren leaned against a building and looked around her. Her eyes circled the milling throngs of holiday shoppers, coming to rest on a pair of laughing, dark eyes across the aisle from where she was standing. She became mesmerized, her breath catching in her throat.

For that one brief moment time stood still as she continued to return Marc Rayven's gaze. The hot sun was now a warm caress; the shrill cries of the vendors became soft words of nothingness. The vibrant colors whispered to her, and the hot, dry wind cloaked her softly. Her heart thumped madly in her breast. This couldn't be happening to her. After that humiliating scene in the garden last night she couldn't be standing here feeling this way. It was insane. She had to get away, she had to move, run. Run! Her mind ordered.

Suddenly, a babble of voices rang through the bazaar as a horde of children raced past the over-crowded stalls. Caren jumped out of the way and then quickly regained her composure. When she looked for Marc again, he was gone. Where was he? Climbing on a stool, she let her eyes rake the customers of the bazaar. He was nowhere about. He was gone! The sun was again a hot, brutal mantle of heat; the shrill cries of the merchants fell tumultuously on her ears and the persistent wind was torturous to her fair skin. She had to leave, to move before he found her. She managed somehow to fight her way through the jostling crowds to an area far removed from the bazaar.

She was angry, her momentary lapse back in the bazaar forgotten. Of course, he was looking for her. He couldn't let her get away from him. She was the goose that was laying the golden eggs. She was what was going to make him _numero uno,_ right up there with Charles Revson. He'd probably even write a book about his experiences sometime and make her a fool in print. She knew she was thinking nasty, terrible things about the man she loved but she couldn't help it. She felt so ashamed to have fallen for his "line" that she felt almost physically sick.

If only she could go back to that pool and sink down into the cool wetness right up to her neck. She felt so hot and weary, so used and abused, that tears again threatened to erupt. Feeling sorry for herself wasn't going to get her anywhere. Midmorning and she still had to trek back to the hotel. What she had to do right now was put one foot in front of the other as fast as she could.

At best it was agonizing torture to walk along the desert road. The temperature, according to her perspiring brow, must be hovering somewhere around one hundred degrees. Her hair hung in limp, wet strands and plastered itself against her sweaty cheeks. Her neck felt stiff and the tiny particles of sand from the hot desert winds were sticking to her, making her itch. Hot, searing anger coursed through her. This discomfort was all Marc Rayven's fault.

The high-pitched whine of a desert jeep made her stop and turn. Well, what else had she expected? she wondered disgustedly. Of course, he would ride. Kings always rode and the stupid subjects walked. She squared her shoulders and continued to trudge down the road, only this time she walked on the side, leaving room for his jeep to pass. She was angry about her appearance, angry with the brutal heat, and angry with the man who was riding in the jeep, looking so cool and aloof. He was saying something. She ignored him.

"Only a fool walks in this heat. Get in and I'll take you back to the hotel. That's an order, Caren."

"Leave me alone."

"Get in before you suffer a heat stroke and I have to put you in a hospital. I won't tell you again. Get in!"

This time it was an iron command and Caren flinched. More anger surged through her. "Oh sure, and then you can take a picture of me spraying Nightstar on myself in a hospital bed. Well, for your information, the only thing I'll be spraying from now on is disinfectant. To get rid of you, Mr. Rayven. Now, leave me alone." She was feeling lightheaded. It must be the anger she was feeling or maybe she was dehydrating. Not knowing anything about dehydration, it seemed as good a reason as any she could think of at the moment. "I'm getting in, but under protest," she said weakly.

"Look at your feet. Why are your toes bleeding?" Marc demanded.

Caren's head buzzed. He could ask the dumbest questions at the dumbest times. Talking seemed such an effort. "For a cosmetics rep, and I use the term lightly, you really are a mess, do you know that? My toes *aren't* bleeding; that's nail polish. Rayven Crimson Berry to be exact." Caren frowned; her voice sounded thick and her tongue felt swollen. "I thought you were offering me a ride, why are we sitting here?"

"I think you've about had it, Caren. The heat can do cruel things to a person. For God's sake if you wanted to go to the damned bazaar, why didn't you take the hotel shuttle or borrow the jeep for that matter?"

"Mr. Rayven, every time I listen to you I manage to get fouled up in some way. You did ask me to get in this jeep so you could drive me back to the hotel? That was some time ago. Are you going to drive or not?"

The jeep roared to life as Marc floored the gas pedal. Caren leaned back against the seat. Maybe she should catch forty winks and she wouldn't have to talk to him. Her last conscious thought as she drifted off was that her big toe was indeed bleeding. Maybe he wasn't so dumb after all.

The jeep hit a deep rut in the road and Caren's eyes flew open. Soon she would have a cold drink and be within the air-conditioned confines of her apartment. The rest would take care of itself. So what if she allowed him to transport her back to the palace-hotel? That was all she was conceding. She risked opening one eye and was chagrined to see mocking eyes staring down at her. Fool! she chided herself.

"You're exhausted, but I knew you weren't out of it. Stop pretending, Caren. It's time you and I had a talk and that's exactly what we're going to do as soon as we get back to the hotel. I'm going to throw you into the pool in my apartment and there's no way you're going to get out till you listen to me. Do you understand what I'm saying?"

"I'm not as stupid as you seem to think," Caren snapped. "That's what hurt the most. The fact that you thought I was so stupid I would fall for all of your tricks. Well, I'm wise to your antics now, so let's continue this ride in silence. There's nothing you can say to me that holds the least bit of interest. I told you I was finished and I meant it."

"Somehow I never thought of you as a quitter, Caren." The words were soft and full of regret.

Caren hardened her heart. "And," she said, a

note of steel in her tone, "I didn't think you were a liar and a trickster. You know all the weasel words, don't you? You have all the traits of the consummate politician. You missed your calling. I'll bet you even kiss babies."

"You are the most stubborn, the most exasperating, the most—"

"I don't want to hear it. That's no more true than all the other things you've been saying about me," Caren interrupted.

"It's not important what you think, not any longer," Marc snapped back, his face furious, his hands tight on the steering wheel. "Okay, we're here. You're going to shut up even if I have to muzzle you. One false move on your part and you've bought it. Do I make myself clear?"

Caren gulped. He couldn't talk to her like this. Of all the insufferable nerve! "And don't get any funny ideas about carrying me. I can walk by myself. I am going to use your pool—alone."

Marc grinned as he waited for her to climb from the jeep. He was next to her, ready to reach for her arm. She jerked free of him and started to walk around the garden, intent only on jumping into the sparkling pool and submerging herself till she was cool and refreshed.

Marc's eyes were laughing as he watched her stand at the edge of the pool. "The way I see it, you have two choices. You can skinny-dip, as we say back home, or you can go in with that silk shirt you're wearing."

He was mocking her again. Did he think she was stupid enough to go about with nothing on beneath the yellow caftan? Evidently, by the leer in his eye, that was exactly what he did think.

"Go away! Go find Moira and tell her some lies like you told me. Make love to her and tell her she's the only woman in the whole world for you. Maybe she's dumb enough to fall for your line, but I don't think so. That one would want it in writing and in triplicate, a copy for her and one for her attorney. If you're lucky she might give you one."

Marc laughed, a great booming sound that seemed to come from his toes. She watched in horror as he slipped off his shoes and socks and started to unbutton his shirt. Her eyes widened as his hands fumbled with his belt. He wouldn't...he wasn't going...

Before she knew what was happening, he was in the water, a flash of bronze skin and then ripples. Had he... Was he down to the buff? She had closed her eyes momentarily, missing the fact that he was wearing swim trunks beneath his slacks. She also didn't notice the dark hand that snaked out over the rim of the pool. Her ankle was in a viselike grip and then she was tumbling into the water, the heavy caftan dragging her down. She struggled to the surface, sputtering and howling. "You...you...war-paint mogul. Stay away from me. How dare you get into this pool without...without...naked! I'll scream. Do you hear me? I'll scream!"

"Go ahead." Marc grinned as he leaned back against the sides of the pool. His dark eyes danced merrily. "I do think, though, we should even up the odds a little." Suddenly, his hand was at the neck of her caftan and the sound of the wet material being ripped was thunderously loud in the stillness that surrounded them. "Now, you won't want to get out for fear I'll see all of your womanly attributes, and I won't want to get out for fear you'll see all of my manly attributes. I think it's called a Mexican standoff."

"You're disgusting," Caren sputtered as she tried to wrap the wet cloth around her, covering her wet, revealing undergarments. He was beneath the water tugging at the material until it was free.

"Now, it's safe to say you're a water nymph. Or a mermaid."

"Where's your stinky perfume? I'm surprised you don't carry a bottle around your neck for emergencies like this," Caren said heatedly. "I'm warning you, stay away from me."

"You're thinking of Saint Bernards." Marc laughed. "You know, they carry brandy and save snowbound and frostbitten people."

"Well, I'm not snowbound and I'm not a nymph and I'm not a mermaid. I'm cool now and I want to get out of here. Turn around."

"Not on your life. I'm staying right here till you turn into a prune. I want to see what you'll look like when you get old. If I'm going to grow old with a woman, the least I should get is a sneak preview."

"Think again, Mr. Rayven. If that was supposed to be some kind of left-handed proposal, I'm rejecting the offer."

"You don't have a choice. As soon as we get back to New York, I plan to marry you."

"Stupid and dumb. I'm not marrying you. I could never again believe anything you told me. I wouldn't marry you if you were the last man on earth."

"If you stay here much longer, I will be. Just

how many men do you think would put up with you? Not many," he said, answering his own question. "You should just see yourself. You're a mess. Only a man in love with you would think you look beautiful. And," he said, wagging a playful finger, "you aren't even wearing my perfume."

"Why should I? It stinks. Did I tell you it S-T-I-N-K-S?"

"Sure, but I didn't believe you. You see, you tell lies to suit your convenience. I thought a small wedding, a hundred or so guests. We could go to the Philippines to finish out the ad campaign and then I'll lock you up somewhere in some white cottage with a picket fence, and we'll have five kids, enough for a basketball team. I like basketball, did I ever tell you that?"

"No, and I'm not interested." She watched in horror as Marc trod water till he was next to her. With virginal modesty she crossed her arms over her breasts and tried to blend into the side of the pool.

"This is ridiculous, all of this game-playing. You know I love you. I've loved you since the first time I saw you in that board meeting. You are a bit of a sow's ear. They're words, Caren— they mean nothing. All the photographers, all of the makeup artists, can't make you something you're not. All they give you is a veneer that washes off. It's what's here," he said, touching her eyelids lightly. "It's what's here," he said tracing his finger down her neck to a place slightly below her breasts. "You fell in love with me long after I fell in love with you. It makes no difference what Moira or Jacques say. It's what *I* say and what *you* say that matters. I love you. That's the bottom line. The game is over now. It's up to you to decide what you want to do. But first, I think you should hear me out, Caren."

"No more lies, Marc. I don't want to hear them."

"I've never lied to you, Caren."

She looked into his eyes, felt herself held in his gaze, and she knew that whatever he would tell her would be truth. She dropped her eyes, quiet, waiting. She felt herself being taken into his arms; his lips were very near her ear, his voice barely more than a whisper.

"Caren, first I must tell you that it was no accident that Maggie Bryant asked you to cover the minutes of the board meeting. I'd noticed you for some time before that. I'd already for-mulated my plan for making you the Nightstar girl. Or at least I was determined to give it an all-American try. I didn't honestly know whether you'd work out or not. Sometimes, the most beautiful women can't project a camera. But I did know that I wanted someone with your qualities; a wholesomeness—Mom and apple pie.... You're what the girl next door grows up to be. To me, that's the finest thing any woman can achieve. That's why I didn't want a glossy high-fashion model. In fact, I wanted you to be the Nightstar girl so much that I didn't dare let my hopes be known. So I downplayed it, too much I'm afraid and even cruelly. I couldn't let anyone know how important you were. But Bill Valenti and Jacques began to suspect that day I barged in on that photo session and saw you with your wrapper dropped off your shoulders and the light playing off your silky skin.... I was jealous, protective—a fool."

Caren felt her heart beat a pace faster. He had said jealous.... "And because you didn't want anyone to know how important my being the Nightstar girl was you called me a sow's ear?" Caren asked, holding her breath for his answer.

"Exactly. Which leads me to Moira. I had no idea that she had tried to sabotage you with Jacques. And I now know that it was Moira who spilled the beans to the press at the film opening. I discovered it only recently. Moira and I go back a long way—all the way to college. I knew she was capable of some dirty tricks, but I never thought she'd stoop so low. Thankfully, Jacques saw his duty to the company, but only because he thinks the world of you, Caren. I've been wrong. I know it. For years I've allowed Moira to daydream about me and our relationship because I didn't think it serious enough to do anything about it. Moira was the best assistant a man could have—''

"Was?" Caren squeaked.

"Yes, was. Moira knew from the beginning how I felt about you, Caren, because I told her. Remember that night in your apartment when I stormed out on you? That was the night I told her. In fact, I thanked her later for calling when she did. I knew I loved you and I wanted you to have a chance to fall in love with me. I didn't want to do anything that would hurt that chance. But, damn it woman, you are the most desirable, most loving, and giving—I almost lost control, almost took advantage of you. I'd been too used to getting what I wanted from a woman. I needed time to cool off and so—''

"There had never been anything between you

and Moira?'' Caren was surprised to find her voice so controlled, so level.

"Only in Moira's head, I'm afraid."

"But I overheard her with you in the garden beneath my hotel room. I saw you hold her—"

"I know what you heard and it was vicious and untrue."

"But I saw—"

"You saw me take her in my arms. I felt sorry for her. I had just told her the truth about how I really feel about you and that I was going to ask you to marry me. I had also just told her that I couldn't work with anyone who was so devious and caused so much pain. Especially when that pain and trickery was directed at the woman I love. And I do love you, Caren. More than words can say."

Splashing and frolicking like two children, they reveled in their newfound closeness. They were standing in waist-high water, and Caren's breasts were firm, their rosy crests erect and hard from the coolness of the pool. She saw Marc's eyes drift to them time and again, his pleasure evidenced by his sultry look.

Once he bent to grasp her knees and pull her down, the water closing over her head. Whooping for revenge, Caren splashed and tormented him by threatening to run from the pool.

Laughing, Marc captured her and threatened to dip her beneath the surface again. Screaming for mercy, Caren clung to him fiercely, her arms locked around his neck, her face pressed close to his. Suddenly time stopped, the birds were silent. Nothing and no one existed in the whole world, save the two of them—two lovers enraptured with each other and reveling in that private world that only those in love can enter.

Gently, he embraced her, cradling her head in one of his hands while the other supported her haunches. Backward, backward, he dipped her. Into her line of vision swept the treetops and the sky, which was darkening by the moment. Slowly, deliberately, he bent his head, beads of water shining on his dark hair. Closer and closer his mouth came to hers. Tighter and tighter became his hold on her, as if he were clinging to her, desperately cleaving to this moment of time, cherishing it, remembering it, burning it into his memory, searing it into his soul.

Caren knew in that moment, without a shred of doubt, that he would cherish her always. She, Caren, the woman she was; her soul, her mind, her body, not the facade in the Nightstar ads.

Caren became his in that one gentle searching kiss, and she knew she could never belong to another.

"Not here, not now," Marc said huskily.

Caren smiled, understanding perfectly. Still, she felt compelled to ask, "When?"

"Later, beneath the first nightstar."

You won't want to miss the newest
hardcover novel that will be on
everyone's lips this summer...

TALK

All of America is tuning in to talk-show diva
Jessica Wright, including a dangerously devoted
secret admirer—a stalker who has planned a finale
even more sensational than any of her shows....

**A novel of intrigue and suspense
from national bestselling author**

LAURA
VAN WORMER

Available in July wherever hardcover books are sold.

MIRA

MLVW317

Her face was a mask
that hid the scars on her soul....

GIRL IN THE MIRROR

Years ago, Charlotte Godowski had become
Charlotte Godfrey at the hands of a brilliant cosmetic
surgeon. She had traded horrified stares for the
adulation of Hollywood, loneliness and mockery for
power, fame and love. She thought she was truly happy
and that her secret could be kept forever—until she
realized that as long as the swan still sees the ugliest of
ducklings in its reflection, so might
the world....

MARY ALICE MONROE

On sale mid-August 1998
where paperbacks are sold!

MIRA®

MMAM451

**The only thing stronger than
Camilla Vane's lust for power and money
is one man's hunger for revenge....**

SCARLET ANGEL

She's a beautiful, ambitious and unscrupulous woman
who finds the perfect power base on George Marchant's
estate. He knows she only married him for his money—
but after causing one divorce, one suicide and one death,
it seems she wants more than the family fortune....

From international bestselling author

ELIZABETH PALMER

On sale mid-July 1998
where paperbacks are sold!

MIRA

Look us up on-line at: http://www.romance.net

MEP456

If you enjoyed this story
of passionate romance
by award-winning author

FERN
MICHAELS

**Don't miss the opportunity to receive her other
title from MIRA® Books:**

#66003	PAINT ME RAINBOWS	$4.99 U.S.☐ $5.50 CAN.☐

(quantities may be limited)

TOTAL AMOUNT	$	
POSTAGE & HANDLING	$	
($1.00 for one book, 50¢ for each additional)		
APPLICABLE TAXES*	$	
TOTAL PAYABLE	$	
(check or money order—please do not send cash)		

To order, complete this form and send it, along with a check or money order for the total above, payable to MIRA Books, to: **In the U.S.:** 3010 Walden Avenue, P.O. Box 9077, Buffalo, NY 14269-9077; **In Canada:** P.O. Box 636, Fort Erie, Ontario L2A 5X3.

Name: _____

Address: _____ City: _____

State/Prov.: _____ Zip/Postal Code: _____

Account Number: _____ (if applicable)   075 CSAS

*New York residents remit applicable sales taxes.
Canadian residents remit applicable GST and provincial taxes.

MIRA BOOKS®

**The Brightest Stars
in Fiction.™**